The Flirt

Also by Marion Chesney in Large Print:

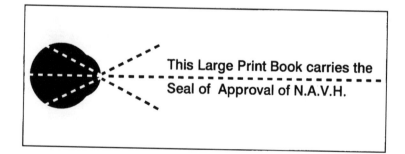

This Large Print Book carries the
Seal of Approval of N.A.V.H.

The Flirt

Marion Chesney

Thorndike Press • Waterville, Maine

Published in 2002 by arrangement with Lowenstein Associates, Inc.

Thorndike Press Large Print Core Series.

The tree indicium is a trademark of Thorndike Press.

The text of this Large Print edition is unabridged.
Other aspects of the book may vary from the original edition.

Cover design by Thorndike Press Staff.

Set in 16 pt. Plantin by Myrna S. Raven.

Printed in the United States on permanent paper.

F
Ches
LARGE PRINT

Library of Congress Cataloging-in-Publication Data

Chesney, Marion.
  The flirt / by Marion Chesney.
    p. cm.
  ISBN 0-7838-9611-5 (lg. print : hc : alk. paper)
  1. Large type books. I. Title.
  PR6053.H4535 F58 2002
  823′.914—dc21
                                                    2001051441

*For my friend
Rachael Feild,
With love*

Chapter One

The ballroom was a swirling kaleidoscope of color and jewels, flowers and candles. Almack's Assembly Rooms at the height of the Season. All the rich and privileged were there, talking, flirting, gossiping.

In the very center of the most exclusive group stood Elizabeth Markham in a gown of gold tissue, her hair dressed *à la Sappho* and little gold sandals on her feet. Although she was only seventeen, her beauty had broken many hearts during the Season. The jealous had labeled her a dangerous flirt. But the fact was that Elizabeth, despite her beauty, did not think much of herself and never took any of her courtiers seriously. For most of her adolescence, she had been a fat little girl and had only recently emerged as a swan. Her fair, almost silver hair gleamed with health, and her wide-spaced blue eyes shone like sapphires. Her admirers competed with each other as to which of them would have the honor of leading her into the waltz, and at last they all fell back and left the field to Lord Charles Lufford. Lord Charles, youngest son of the duke of Dunster, was a noted leader of the ton, and some said his power was greater than Mr. Brummell's. He was a tall elegant man in his midthirties, with jet-black hair and vivid green eyes that looked out on the world with a mocking gaze.

He was said to be the only man in London who had not fallen victim to the bewitching Miss Markham's beauty.

She had always been aware of him. Although he irritated her with that lazy mocking air of his, he was undoubtedly the most handsome man on the London scene. It piqued her that he should seem to remain so indifferent to her and would not play the same flirtatious game as her other suitors. For although in her heart Elizabeth did not take any of her suitors' compliments seriously, at the same time she craved their praise, always fearful she would look in her glass and find she had changed back into the former dumpy and plain Elizabeth of such a short time ago.

"Are you determined to break all the hearts in London, Miss Markham?" he teased. "There is only one day of the Season left, and you have still to break mine."

"Yours is said to be unbreakable, my lord."

"Perhaps. But have you no pity for those you *do* break?"

"If they really broke, I would weep. But the gentlemen only *pretend* to admire me. This Season I am the fashion. They will find another belle the next."

"So young and so cynical. What of young Cartwright, gone to the wars because you rejected his suit?"

Elizabeth gave an infinitesimal shrug. "I think you will find he really wanted to go. He put it about it was because of me. It is tonish to act so."

"One of these days, Miss Markham," he said severely, "your heart will break, and *then* you will remember the Cartwrights of this world with pity."

The colors of the ballroom and the voices faded and swirled off into the mists of memory. A chill northern wind blew down the bleak cobbled street. Elizabeth shivered and drew her shawl more closely about her shoulders.

She must stop retreating into the past. It only made the pain of the present more acute. She was no longer the reigning petted and feted belle of London society but Miss Elizabeth Markham, poor relation and spinster of the parish.

Her heart had not been broken by any man but by the cruelty of her relations.

On the day after that last ball, her parents had been killed. Her father had been driving her mother in his racing curricle. He had never been a good driver or a good judge of horse-flesh, and his mettlesome team had bolted. The carriage had shivered to pieces. Her mother had broken her neck, and her father had been dragged along the ground in his desperate efforts to stop his team. He had lived only a few hours after his wife.

The jewels and the clothes, the house in the

country, and the house in London all went under the hammer to pay the spendthrift Markham couple's debts. The only relative prepared to give a home to Elizabeth was her uncle Julius, her father's brother, a dissenting minister who lived in the town of Bramley, Yorkshire.

Julius Markham was a grim, sour-faced man who lived with an equally sour-faced wife and two spiteful daughters in a cold square barracks of a house in the center of the town.

He had long despised his brother's profligate mode of life and was determined to apply the lash of Christianity to Elizabeth's back in order to flog out all of the seven deadly sins she had obviously inherited in full measure from her parents.

At first she had rebelled. She had cried and screamed when all her pretty clothes and few remaining trinkets were shut away in the attic. As a punishment she had been locked in her room and starved until she repented. Elizabeth had only pretended to repent, determined to get her own way in the end. But as dreary day followed dreary day, as the burden of parish visiting was thrust upon her, her spirit began to break, and she longed for each night to come so that she could lose herself in sleep.

Two years had passed since that London Season. Two years of drudgery and cruelty. She had been put into black mourning clothes and, it seemed, was never to be allowed out of them.

Her once-fashionably cut hair was now long and severely braided on top of her head, her white-gold locks hidden under a depressing bonnet shaped like a coal scuttle.

That one golden memory of the ball had come flying in from the moors on the first breath of spring wind. How casual and flighty I was, thought Elizabeth with a sort of wonder. If only I could have foreseen the future, then I would have married the first man who asked me.

During that Season, she had pitied the girls who *had* to marry before the end of it in order to justify the horrendous expense. Although Elizabeth accepted that all women were expected to marry as early as possible, she had somehow dreamt that things in her case would be different, that she would be able to pick and choose. Other debutantes might marry for money, for safety, or the freedom from strict social laws imposed on all virgins but not she.

She hesitated on the doorstep of Number 7 Glebe Street, reluctant to enter. Mrs. Battersby lived at Number 7 along with her drunken husband and her six children. A year ago, before she had entered Mr. Markham's church, she had been a rosy, rather slatternly country-woman, amused at her husband's drunken bouts rather than outraged.

But Mr. Markham had persuaded her that there would be no place in Heaven for her or her children if she did not reform her husband.

She had gradually turned into a bitter, nagging woman, and the more she nagged, the more guilty her husband became, and the more guilty he became, the more he drank.

And the more Mrs. Battersby complained, the more it seemed she was regarded as a true member of the church.

Elizabeth closed her eyes and knocked at the door, praying that she might manage to cut the visit as short as possible.

She could see the purpose of visits to the poor with clothes or visits to the sick with cordials and medicine, but a visit to a poor tortured woman for the sole purpose of reporting her failure to sober her husband to Mr. Markham seemed cruel and useless. Elizabeth would gladly have lied had Mrs. Battersby wished it, but Mrs. Battersby had become that most unsympathetic of creatures, a self-ordained martyr, and she would not have thanked Elizabeth one little bit for having taken the edge off her martyrdom.

Mrs. Battersby herself opened the door and invited Elizabeth in with a jerk of her head. "He's here," she said with gloomy relish. The Battersbys lived in the small dark bottom half of a house. Living room and bedroom were combined, the sleeping quarters being one large bed set into a recess in the wall in which all eight Battersbys slept together. The children, ages six to sixteen, were all out working at the wool manufactury. It was not so much the amount Mr. Battersby spent on gin that kept the family in such abysmal poverty but the amount Mrs. Battersby gave to the church. She had obviously never looked at the framed text Charity Begins at Home that ornamented the wall over the bed.

Mr. Battersby was seated at a table in the center of the room, his head pillowed in his arms. A cloud of blue despair engendered by hangover and wifely nagging seemed to hover over his head.

Mrs. Battersby was still wearing the country dress she had worn as a girl; short basqued bodice, petticoat, and a folded handkerchief draped over head under a black square-crowned felt hat.

"He's done it again," she said, folding her hands over her bosom and looking at her husband with grim satisfaction, "and so I shall tell Mr. Markham come Sunday."

"It says in the Bible," said Elizabeth timidly, "that we should learn to turn the other cheek."

"It says," said Mrs. Battersby, "in the Psalms, 'Upon the ungodly He shall rain snares, fire and brimstone, storm and tempest; this shall be their portion to drink.'"

"Oh, dear," said Elizabeth, having a ludicrous vision of poor Mr. Battersby cowering under a storm of bear traps and rabbit snares. She said aloud, "I am come to ask you, as usual, if we can expect to see Mr. Battersby in church."

"Ask him," said Mrs. Battersby grimly. "Miss

do be speaking to you," she said to her husband, shouting so loudly that one of the neighbors hammered on the wall.

"I ain't a sinner," said Mr. Battersby, raising his heavy head and disclosing a swollen and purple face. "It's that Markham what's the sinner. Him and his hellfire. There ain't been a bit o' peace in this house since Martha was took by the church. I ain't going to be preachified at; and so you can tell him." He got to his feet.

"Where are you going?" screamed his wife.

"Out," he snarled, "to get drunk."

"Stop him," yelled Mrs. Battersby. She threw herself in front of her husband and spat full in his face. Like an enraged bull, he lashed out at her with such force that she shot backward across the room and fell, hitting her head on the fender with a sickening crack.

Elizabeth rushed forward to help her, feeling sick, feeling sure the blow had killed her. But Mrs. Battersby lunged to her feet, thrust Elizabeth aside, and tore out into the street after her husband, where she could be heard shouting, "Strike me, would you? Hit me again. That's what you want to do, isn't it. *Isn't it?* Hit me. Go on. *Hit me!*"

There was the sound of a scuffle and then a thump. Mrs. Battersby came back a few minutes later, holding her eye. "That'll be real black by Sunday. Wait till they sees it," she said with satisfaction. She seemed to be enjoying

14

herself, to have had some sort of release caused by her husband's violence.

"Now, miss," she went on cheerfully, "why don't you read me a bit of the Psalms while I get on with my cleaning."

"Very well." Elizabeth took her Bible out of her reticule. Mrs. Battersby was always scouring some part of the house with such ferocity that Elizabeth sometimes thought it a miracle that the whole place wasn't erased, simply rubbed out, leaving a gap like a lost tooth in the row of houses.

As she read, she noticed the way Mrs. Battersby's lips moved soundlessly. She was probably rehearsing what she would say next Sunday.

Then, as she read, Elizabeth found the face of Lord Charles Lufford rising before her mind's eye. His father, the duke of Dunster, had estates about twenty miles outside the town. When she had first come to Bramley, Elizabeth used to dream that Lord Charles would drive through the town, see her, and promptly demand her hand in marriage. She could well imagine Lord Charles's cool and mocking air putting her uncle firmly in his place. But no such rescuer rode to her side, and after a while, she ceased to dream, for the temporary escape supplied by fantasies made the return to harsh reality all the more unpleasant.

Then she frowned. Lord Charles had not been numbered among her suitors, therefore why should she now think of him? The only reason she had thought of him two years ago was because there was a possibility she might see him should he visit his father.

"Go on," admonished Mrs. Battersby, and Elizabeth blushed, realizing she had stopped reading.

The sun was dying at the end of the street when she left, going down over Bramley in a blaze of yellow glory, washing the cobbles with gold and gilding the chimneypots. Blackbirds were caroling from the rooftops, and there was that seductive smell of spring in the air.

For the first time in two years, Elizabeth began to feel a tiny spark of rebellion. There must be some way to escape. If only she had known what was going to happen that sunny Season that now seemed so very long ago. She would have married *anyone*. Why had she not been like the other girls? Why had she not accepted the reality that marriage was the only future for a gentlewoman?

She pushed open the tall iron gates that led to Chuff House, which was the name of the Markham residence. She had never found out whether a family called Chuff had once lived there or whether it was a local word now fallen into disuse. Chuff seemed too friendly and warm a name for the tall, grim, brick mansion facing her.

She rang the bell — she was not allowed a key — and the door was answered by Perkins. Perkins was a tall, grim-faced northern woman who had worked as parlor-maid-cum-housemaid for the Markhams for the past twenty years. She crackled with starch. The streamers of her cap were so starched that they stuck out rigidly over the knot of hair at the back of her neck.

Elizabeth asked her to take her cloak and shawl, but Perkins stalked off, affecting not to hear. Although Mr. Markham's two daughters, Patience and Prudence, were waited on hand and foot, it was understood among the servants that Miss Elizabeth must shift for herself.

Elizabeth put her cloak and shawl in the cloakroom and went upstairs to wash her hands before supper. She stood at the bedroom window for a moment looking out. The moors rose gently above the town, a green-and-brown patchwork under the setting sun. A messenger boy strolled along the street below, his hands thrust in his pockets, whistling loudly.

The garden below was as ordered and chastised as the souls of Mr. Markham's flock. Sooty laurels struggled up from their bed of gravel to crouch against the iron railings. A line of pollarded elms decorated the front, and the few flower beds were kept from any temptation to riot by prim borders of clam-shells and green shards of broken bottles.

Elizabeth watched until the very last bit of sun had sunk below the horizon and the clamor of the supper bell sounded from downstairs.

The Markham family was already seated at

the table when Elizabeth slipped quietly into the dining room. Mr. Markham sat at the head of the table. He was a tall man who looked smaller because of a perpetual stoop. His face was very white against the rusty black of his clericals, and he had rather protruding pale blue eyes. Mrs. Markham, who sat at the opposite end of the table, was small and dumpy, the roundness of her country features being marred by a bristling orange-red mustache. Elizabeth still remembered her own surprised laughter on her arrival when she had first seen that mustache. She had thought Mrs. Markham was a jolly sort of woman whose idea of fun was to put on a false mustache. Mrs. Markham had been outraged at what she called Elizabeth's deliberate impertinence, but her outrage had not made her shave it off.

Patience and Prudence were younger versions of their mother. Both had fizzed and teased orange-red hair. Prudence, at twenty-one, was older than Patience by a year, and her upper lip had a soft orange bloom on it, harbinger of the middle-aged mustache to come. Both girls were great gigglers. They always seemed to be laughing at someone else, and so their giggles had a spiteful edge. They were both finely if unfashionably dressed in the same pattern of gowns and the same color of ribbons by the town dressmaker. Mrs. Markham had dressed them alike since the day Patience was born and was proud when people thought they were twins, as though delivering herself of a double burden of baby had been something rare and wonderful. The female side of the Markham family did not share Mr. Markham's religious fanaticism, and strangely enough, he did not seem to expect them to do so. Patience and Prudence were often absent from church because of various minor ailments, and Mrs. Markham had the Headache — her prime weapon — which had served her so far from attending too many church services and from bearing any more children.

Although the Markhams were gentry, their tastes and companions hailed from the middle class of the town.

Supper consisted of damson pie, pork pie, mutton steaks, hot mashed potatoes, puffs, brawn, and cold roast beef.

Elizabeth was very hungry. She wondered whether to rebel and serve herself as the members of the Markham family were doing, but that would mean bread and water for days as a punishment. It had been made plain to Elizabeth from the day of her arrival that she should wait patiently until Mrs. Markham finally decided to give her a little food from the spread on the table.

Did Mrs. Markham suspect or *sense* that spark of rebellion inside Elizabeth that was slowly growing into a flame? Perhaps it was the new glow in Elizabeth's large blue eyes, eyes that looked too large for her thin face, that caused Mrs. Markham to give her less than usual.

There was no friendly servant in the house to take Elizabeth's side. The small staff had been in residence long before Elizabeth's arrival. They knew better than to risk losing their jobs over one poor relation.

Elizabeth ate her food, carefully chewing every mouthful slowly to make it last.

Then she heard Patience say, "The tradespeople are in a great flutter. It seems the duke of Dunster is having a grand house party and all the lords and ladies are traveling up from London. There is to be a great ball. Some of the local gentry have already been invited."

"We will not go," said Mr. Markham solemnly. "Dancing is one of the tools of the devil."

Patience looked down at her plate, quickly covering up her obvious disappointment by saying sanctimoniously, "You are right, of course, Papa. I am sure Elizabeth would like to go. *She* was always dancing when she was in London."

Mr. Markham's pale eyes rested on Elizabeth's face. "Elizabeth has learned the folly of her ways," he said. "She would not accept such an invitation."

"There is no question of accepting or refusing an invitation," said Elizabeth. "Dissenting ministers and their families are beyond the social pale."

"Where we are pleased to be," said Mr. Markham, his voice rising. "I do not like your tone of voice, Elizabeth. It smacks of impertinence. Go to your room and memorize Psalm One hundred-twelve, and you will come to my study in the morning and repeat it. Where would the poor be were it not for people like myself?"

"A great deal better off," Elizabeth heard herself say. "There are many evangelicals who do great work for the poor, that I admit. It can be argued, however, that religious men such as yourself often plan a better future for the poor in the next world rather than this."

"Go to your room," shouted Mr. Markham, "and stay there until you are prepared to get down on your knees before me and offer me a humble apology!"

With her head held high, Elizabeth marched out of the room and upstairs.

But half an hour of solitude saw her burst of rebellion ebb away, leaving her hungry and frightened. She would be punished. There would be nothing but bread and water for days. She would finally be forced to humiliate herself.

She cried bitterly and long, grieving for her happy, frivolous parents now under the cold ground.

One by one the Markhams and their servants went to bed. Elizabeth sat in a hard upright chair by the window, too hungry to feel sleepy.

Her hunger was exacerbated by the thought of the days of bread and water to follow.

The door of her room was not locked because the Markhams knew very well she had nowhere to escape to.

And then she thought of that ball at the duke of Dunster's. How she would love to go! If only she could have one evening's frivolity away from this grim house with its smells of cabbage water and sanctimony.

Her stomach gave an angry rumble, and her eyes began to fill again with tears. She brushed them away impatiently with the back of her hand.

Then a little voice began to nag in her brain. "If you are going to be confined to bread and water for the next few days — and you know you *will* be, even if you do repent — then why not commit the ultimate sin of going down to the kitchens and *stealing* something."

Elizabeth raised her hands to her hot cheeks. Stealing was a crime. "Stealing, in this case, is a necessity," jeered the little voice.

Elizabeth rose abruptly to her feet and walked like a marionette to the door. She made her way downstairs, now thinking of nothing else but getting into the kitchen and finding something to eat.

The candle in her hand did not waver. Not even when she put it down on the kitchen table and turned to examine the shelves in the pantry did she pause to think of the enormity of what she was doing.

She cut two thick slices of bread and made a sandwich with a generous amount of roast beef. She drew herself a tankard of beer from the barrel in the corner of the kitchen, thinking it an odd paradox that beer was allowed downstairs but considered the devil's broth above. Then she ate the rest of the damson pie, after which she began to pile a tray high with various sorts of food to fortify her for the long fast ahead. It was only when she had finally undressed and was climbing into bed that she realized she did not feel guilty and that the considerable amount she had eaten had, in fact, wiped out any remaining guilt that might still have been hovering around.

There would be other ways, she thought sleepily, in which she could make her life comfortable if only she began to show a little bit more courage.

She was awakened by Betsy the chambermaid coming in to open the curtains and take away the slops, two of the menial jobs Elizabeth was not asked to do, although she was expected to see to the rest of the cleaning of her room herself.

She had hidden the stolen food in the bottom of the wardrobe. Among it was a piece of garlicky sausage, and she saw Betsy sniffing the air suspiciously before she left.

Elizabeth decided to have the garlic sausage for breakfast.

At ten o'clock Mr. Markham sent word that

the family would be out all day and she was not even to have bread and water.

Elizabeth was amazed that he should think her so cowed as to not dare to leave her room, until she remembered that her behavior since her arrival two years earlier had been so meek, so frightened, and so subservient that he had every reason to believe she would be too terrified to move an inch.

After a while she crossed to the window and watched them all drive away. For a while she could hear the maids going about the house cleaning and dusting. Then there was silence.

Outside, a lively spring wind was tearing through the town and out across the moors. Elizabeth longed to be able to go out and walk on the moors. At least she was not expected to do any parish visiting while she was in disgrace, but it would be fun to walk and walk across those moors away from the house.

If she simply walked downstairs and out of the door, it was doubtful if the servants would try to stop her, as they were all women, Mr. Markham holding the view that male servants were unnecessarily expensive and more able to find other jobs if they were discontented.

Elizabeth went to the window again. It was a pity her room was at the front of the house, she reflected. At the back there was a rusty iron ladder that ran from the roof to the ground, a fire escape to be used in time of need, but as it went straight down to the ground, passing only

Mr. and Mrs. Markham's window, it would not serve as a help to anyone else. Still, she could perhaps have climbed up to the roof and made her way along to it.

But I could make my way *over* the roof, she thought. Her room was on the second floor, so she would have to climb only one story to reach the roof. Her cloak was downstairs, but there was an old black wool spencer in her wardrobe that would serve to keep her warm. She tied a scarf over her head so that anyone seeing her might take her for one of the mill workers.

Then she opened the window and climbed out, balancing herself on the sill and grasping hold of the drainpipe. She took a quick look down and shuddered. The ground seemed such a very long way away.

There was the sound of a carriage approaching, coming along the road that ran outside the house. She would soon be in full view of the occupants of the carriage. But if she climbed back in that window, Elizabeth felt sure that she would never again have the courage to climb out.

She seized the drainpipe and began to climb.

Lord Charles Lufford, who was driving his own team, slowed his traveling carriage to a halt. "Do you think she is breaking in?" he asked his friend Mr. Bertram Seymour. "Looks to me as if she's climbing *out*," said Mr. Seymour, leaning forward on the box to get a better look.

The slim figure in the black dress gained a footing on the roof. Then her foot slipped, and Mr. Seymour let out a gasp. "She'll fall," he said. "We'd better do something. I'll shout. . . ."

"No, she's all right," said Lord Charles. "If you shout, you might startle her." As they watched, the figure gained the ridgepole of the high, sloping roof and then disappeared over the other side.

Mr. Seymour heaved a sigh of relief. "Well, that's that — unless she falls down the other side. Should we report the matter to the parish constable?"

Lord Lufford shook his head. There had been something about the figure of the girl on the roof, something about the turn of her head, that had reminded him of Elizabeth Markham. He wanted to forget that flighty girl, who was probably now married, although no announcement had appeared in the social columns. Her parents' debts had been well publicized, but he had not feared for Elizabeth. That totally selfish young miss would know how to land on her feet. It was amazing how the memory of her could still irritate him.

He gave an impatient shrug, set his team in motion, and firmly put all memories of Elizabeth Markham out of his mind.

Elizabeth ran lightly away from the house, keeping to the back lanes until she was well clear of the town.

Once out on the moors, she removed her

scarf and let the wind blow through her hair. She had not braided it that morning, and it flew out about her in a golden cloud.

She began to run again, enjoying her burst of freedom, going on and up over the moors until the town of Bramley lay at her feet.

She lay down on a tussock of grass and hugged her knees. The enormity of what she had done hit her with full force. The servants would find the missing food and an investigation would start. The slices of roast beef and the bread might have gone unnoticed, but not the damson pie and the other delicacies she had taken to her room.

She wondered what her uncle would do. He would probably birch her in front of the household, a punishment he had inflicted on her for her earlier rebellion. He had certainly not done so since — her screams of outrage had caused the neighbors to come running, and although her uncle was within his rights to beat her if he chose, he had received a great deal of criticism and had confined his punishments to starvation ever since.

And then, all at once, the fear left her. She did not care anymore. She simply did not care anymore. They could beat her, starve her, humiliate her, but she had become used to all of that.

Mr. Markham did not want to turn her out of doors. She knew that. He loved to talk long and loudly about his magnanimity in rescuing his profligate brother's only child.

Entering the town on the white ribbon of road below her was a carriage, the sun glinting on a gilded crest on the panel. Liveried outriders rode alongside. Behind the coach came another carriage, the roof piled high with luggage. The guests were arriving for the house party, thought Elizabeth. She lay back in the grass and gazed up at the drifting clouds, imagining what it would be like to be one of them again, to be part of that glittering social world.

A haunting waltz tune drifted through her mind. The sun was warm on her face. Her eyes began to close, and soon she was asleep.

She awoke three hours later. A chill wind was whispering through the bracken on the moor, and large black clouds were building up to the west.

Fear clutched her heart. Her earlier courage had fled. She got to her feet and began to run, tumbling and stumbling down from the moors to where the town lay sprawled below.

There was no hope of creeping back into the house the way she had left. Dusk had fallen, and lights blazed at every window. Servants were running hither and thither. As she turned into the road that led to the back of the house, hoping still that she might find a way to get in unobserved, Mrs. Battersby appeared at her side.

"They're waiting for you," she said with grim satisfaction. "I told Mr. Markham I saw you up on the moors, running about like a gypsy. I told him when I saw you head this way. Stealing, he says. That be a mortal sin."

She had grasped Elizabeth's arm as she spoke and was looking up into her face with an avid, greedy look.

Elizabeth tore free from her grasp, and instead of continuing on her way to the back of the house, she turned down along the narrow lane that led back around to the front of the house. She might as well take what was coming to her and get it over with as quickly as possible.

They were waiting for her on the step, all the members of the Markham family.

Elizabeth turned white as their shrill voices rose and fell about her ears. The stolen food had been discovered in her wardrobe. Bad blood ran in her veins. She was a limb of Satan.

Prudence and Patience pushed and pummeled her as she was half dragged into Mr. Markham's study. Elizabeth had been so sure he would never dare beat her again. But he went straight to the corner where the birch rod stood and picked it up.

The next fifteen minutes were a dizzying horror of pain and humiliation. Sore and beaten, Elizabeth was finally marched upstairs to her room, and this time the key was turned in the door.

She lay facedown on the bed, too broken in spirit even to cry. One fleeting little thought came into her brain. Would Lord Charles think of her at all when he danced at that ball? And then roaring pain and anguish came down on her again, and she closed her eyes tightly, willing herself to sleep.

Chapter Two

The members of Mr. Markham's flock re-marked with satisfaction that Miss Elizabeth Markham was a changed girl. The other towns-people shrugged and said sadly that old Markham had beaten her down at last. She may have been meek before, but now she lacked even the breath of spirit. She crawled about the town with her head bent, visiting the sick, preaching to the poor, who would rather have had food than words, urging Mr. Battersby to come to church. All this she did like a puppet. During the seven long days after her beating, she walked through a strange twilight world, barely taking in her surroundings. If she thought at all, it was only that she would never, ever again dare to do anything to bring the wrath of her uncle down on her head.

Members of the house party could still be seen, either driving through the town on their way to the duke's or, those who were already established, brightening the dark shops of Bramley with their bright clothes and jewels.

And then, at the end of the seventh day, as Elizabeth was making her way back to Chuff House after her calls, an open carriage bearing five young debutantes stopped beside her. The coachman climbed down to examine one of the traces. Glancing up, Elizabeth recognized two of them from the old London days. They were laughing and giggling, and one was making mock bets about which one of them would win the flinty heart of Lord Charles Lufford.

"He is too old for *me*," said a pretty brunette. "Sally Harper," thought Elizabeth with a kind of wonder, "and still looking exactly the same."

"After all," went on Sally with a toss of her head, "he is thirty-five, and if a man is not wed by that great age, he is never going to marry."

Another of the girls that Elizabeth recognized, Frederica Spencer, said, "He is not too old for me. Faith, he is handsome. I wager my diamond pin I can get him to dance with me *twice*."

Another of the girls tittered, " 'Tis said he showed an interest in Elizabeth Markham, but she is gone away to stay with relatives and has not been seen this age."

Elizabeth stiffened at the sound of her own name. She felt she should move away in case any of them recognized her, but somehow her feet seemed rooted to the ground.

"What is that card in your hand, Sally?" Frederica asked.

"A card to the ball, which was to go to Annabelle Pomfret. But she has the *mumps*, although it is supposed to be a deadly secret. I told the duchess Annabelle would not be able to attend, and she told me to throw the card away, but I put it in my reticule and only remembered it just now."

"Then throw it away," laughed Frederica. She looked down from the carriage and saw Elizabeth who was standing with her head averted. "Throw it to that peasant woman. She will probably *frame* it." The other girls burst out laughing. The coachman climbed back on the box. Sally tossed the invitation in the air, and it fell at Elizabeth's feet.

She bent to pick it up as the carriage bowled away.

"Peasant woman, indeed," thought Elizabeth bitterly. "Was I ever as heedless as that? Did I ever talk about the lower orders as if they did not exist?"

She turned the large gilt-embossed invitation over in her hand. "Well, you wanted an invitation," mocked a voice in her head, "and now you have one."

Elizabeth slid it into her shabby reticule and walked slowly homeward.

Although she had not been confined to her room after her beating, she had been put on that diet of bread and water. Her shabby black clothes hung on her thin frame, and she felt pinched with cold although the day was quite warm.

The invitation in her bag was not only to the ball but to the house party as well. At that party, thought Elizabeth wistfully, there would be mountains and mountains of food. Her mouth began to water.

"If that invitation had been for me," she thought, "I could have gone. My clothes are still in the attic."

Elizabeth had thought she would never have the courage to contemplate escaping from Chuff House again, but all at once her meekness fled, leaving her with one single, burning desire. Somehow she must get to that house party and *eat*. No longer did she think of pretty dresses or of dancing with Lord Charles. She simply thought of being able to eat as much as she wanted.

Thoughts began to scramble about her brain. A great many invitations must have been sent out. If she changed the name on the invitation to that of her own, would they deny her admittance?

No one knew of her fall from society, only that she had left London to stay with relatives. No one knew just how unfashionable those relatives were.

Now if she changed the invitation, if . . . let's dream . . . she planned to go, how to get into the attic? The keys were in the kitchen, but if she managed to get them and get her clothes, how could she reach the duke's without a carriage? She could walk, but everyone would be shocked and amazed if she arrived on foot. She could, of course, say her carriage had crashed and that her servants would be following and hope that everyone would not remark on her absence of servants in the days to come.

Thin as she was, altered in appearance as she was, she must get to that party. Once there, she would let the future take care of itself.

But she knew, all the same, that all these plots and plans were mere fantasy. As the shadow of the house fell across her, her small stock of courage fizzled and died.

She sat with her head bent at the supper table as her portion of bread and a glass of water were put in front of her. She paid no heed to the Markham family conversation until she became aware that Mr. Markham was boasting of the visiting preacher who was to grace his church on Sunday. It was to be a great affair, and the servants were to be allowed to attend as well.

"But who's to mind the house, Papa?" demanded Patience.

"Elizabeth," he said heavily. "Such treats are not for her until she has learned to mend her ways."

Elizabeth could feel hope and excitement bubbling up inside her. She kept her eyes lowered in case any of them might guess her thoughts.

Sunday! An empty house. She would need to escape then if she were ever going to escape at all.

For the next few days Elizabeth was happy, although she hid that fact very well. While Sunday was still in the offing, she could persuade herself that she was actually going to go through with it.

But when Sunday arrived, she had to fight down all sorts of terrors. What if the duchess knew very well that she was staying with her uncle who was that anathema to the ton, a dissenting minister? What if her grace should know that Miss Markham had not been sent an invitation? — even though the list would be sent out by the duke's secretary. Her grace had certainly been aware that Miss Pomfret was on that list and could not attend.

Even when the Markhams and their servants finally left, Elizabeth was almost sure she could not get away with it. But she decided to try. She could always change her mind at the last minute.

She took out the invitation and worked carefully at erasing Annabelle Pomfret's name with a piece of bread saved from her supper. It seemed to take a long time before the inked script began to fade. Then she carefully wrote her own name on the card instead.

She took the keys from the kitchen and climbed up the stairs and unlocked the attic. All her pretty clothes lay packed there. A lump came to her throat as she remembered her flighty, frivolous lady's maid, Belinda, packing away each gown in tissue paper. Where was Belinda now? And all her father's other servants?

She gently took out the ball gown of gold

tissue. As soon as she had done that, she realized she really meant to go through with it, and she began to work like lightning. She donned a fashionable walking dress and a mantle and a pair of bronze kid half boots. Then she packed as many of her clothes as she could into two small sturdy trunks, cording them neatly and twisting the cord to make a handle.

She could say the rest of her luggage must have been left in that mythical carriage with the mythical lady's maid that had met with that mythical accident.

Time had passed quicker than she had realized, and it was only when she was finally closing the house door behind her that she heard the rumble of wheels announcing the Markham family's return from church.

She fled into the darkness of the garden, her trunks bumping against her side, and crouched in the blackness by the railings just as the Markham carriage bowled into the short drive at the front of the house.

She stayed where she was, knowing the servants would shortly be returning on foot and not wanting to risk meeting any of them on the road. She had locked the attic and returned the keys to their place in the kitchen. She had stuffed her charity blacks, dress, shawl, and bonnet under the mattress so they might think these were the clothes she had been wearing when she had made her escape. She had made a dummy of herself on the bed with a bolster and a mop. With any luck her disappearance would not be noticed until the following morning.

The servants arrived at last, Perkins leading the way. Elizabeth counted them as they went past, waiting until she was sure even the pot boy had gone into the house.

Then she picked up her trunks and made her way out onto the road. Twenty miles of walking lay ahead of her, but the exhilaration of freedom lent her feet wings.

It was only when she reached the West Lodge of the duke of Dunster's estate that she suddenly felt weak and shaken. Her head swam with fatigue and lack of food.

There was a small moon riding high above. The night was very still. An owl hooted from the woods in the estate, and a rabbit bounced across the road.

She sank down onto the grass outside the gates, feeling her legs trembling with fatigue.

Elizabeth all at once knew that the duchess would never believe her story, simply because the duchess would know no card had been sent to her.

If by any chance they believed her story of a broken carriage and lost servants, then they would send out *their* servants to scour the countryside and alert the authorities, and soon they would find out she had run away from her uncle's home.

She heard a carriage approaching, but she

was too weary to move.

Nearer it came, the carriage lights bobbing through the dark like two red eyes, the torches of the outriders smoking and flaring. The coach came to a stop outside the gates.

The carriage window was jerked down, and the plump, puzzled face of a lady looked down at Elizabeth sitting on the ground.

"Bless my soul," she said. " 'Tis a young lady! Sitting on the grass! What has happened, miss? Are you ill?"

Elizabeth raised her head wearily and recognized with a start a friend of her late mother's, a Mrs. Burlington, remembering her as a gossipy, silly, kind lady.

She forced herself to get to her feet, hanging onto the side of the carriage for support. "It is I, Elizabeth Markham," she said.

"So it is! So it is! Mr. Burlington," called Mrs. Burlington over her plump shoulder, "you will never believe this, but here is Sophy Markham's daughter, standing right next to me."

A sleepy rumble answered her from the depths of the carriage.

"But what are you doing there, my dear child?" asked Mrs. Burlington.

"My carriage overturned," said Elizabeth, "so I decided to walk. I did not realize it was so far."

"Then isn't it a mercy we found you, for it is still a very long way through the grounds until we reach Hatton Court." Hatton Court was the name of the duke of Dunster's country home.

"Come along," urged Mrs. Burlington. Elizabeth noticed the lodgekeeper coming to open the gates. Summoning up her strength, she climbed into the carriage.

"Good evening," murmured Mr. Burlington sleepily. He was a tall, thin, spare man, a contrast to his plump, fussy wife. Elizabeth sank back wearily against the upholstery of the carriage.

"You are obviously exhausted," said Mrs. Burlington. "What ever became of you? I heard that Julius Markham had taken you north. He is a bishop or something like that, is he not?"

"Yes," mumbled Elizabeth wearily, "something like that."

"And does he not let you do the Season?"

"No, Mrs. Burlington. He does not go to town."

"Such a pity. You have been sorely missed. I was monstrous shocked over your parents' death. Poor Sophy," sighed Mrs. Burlington. "So lively and pretty and gay. Now I must look for my invitation card. The duke gave a rout in London last year, and there were at least five gate-crashers. He is very strict about guests having their cards."

Elizabeth knew now that she simply could not produce that forged card. All she could do was see if they would let her stay the night, and then she would force herself to return to her uncle's.

"I have lost mine," she said in a small voice.

"Well, that is no great matter," said Mrs. Burlington, triumphantly holding up her own invitation. "Our one says 'Mr. and Mrs. Burlington and *party*' because we had some guests staying with us, but they left a while ago, so of course, you can be our party and that will save you explaining matters to a lot of servants. Servants these days are a *plague,* Miss Markham. The ones at our townhouse were so insolent and rude and uppity they frightened us to death. So then Mr. Burlington saw this advertisement from an agency that promised to rid any genteel family of unwanted persons, and so we hired *them.* Do you know they got rid of *every single one!*

"The only trouble was that they replaced them with their own people, who all looked as if they hailed from a thieves' kitchen and who were *much worse* than the old servants. Mr. Burlington was at his wit's end, were you not, my love? We dare not say anything to them for fear of being murdered in our beds. But Mr. Burlington told Lord Charles Lufford of our predicament, and he told us to be absent from the house when he called. When we returned, he had sent them *all* packing. He would not say how he had done it — you know how he is. His agent engaged new staff for us, a treasure each one, I can assure you. Does your uncle have much trouble with his servants?"

"No, none at all," said Elizabeth faintly.

"Ah, well, perhaps bishops' servants are not so worldly as the other kind. The bishop of Bath and Wells was saying to me just the other day that his servants were the most God-fearing creatures and put him quite to shame, but then he is *such* a modest man. What is Mr. Markham bishop *of?*"

"We are nearly there, are we not?" asked Elizabeth, pretending not to hear.

"Are we? Your eyes must be very sharp. I cannot see a thing. You must give me your address, Miss Markham, and I will write to your uncle and beg him to let you come on a little visit to us."

"Do you live near?" asked Elizabeth.

"Not very far. A matter of thirty miles to the west. We sent our servants and luggage ahead. Where did you say your carriage had over-turned?"

"I didn't. . . . I . . ."

"Well, never mind, for I declare you appear a great deal shocked by the accident, and I am sure my talking is giving you the headache, for Mr. Burlington always says it gives *him* one. So now I shall be quiet."

Mrs. Burlington leaned her head back and closed her eyes. "Of course," she went on just as Elizabeth was heaving a sigh of relief, "I rattle on so, I quite forgot to ask you if you were married."

"No, Mrs. Burlington."

"That's a wonder. I 'member saying to Mr.

Burlington, 'Elizabeth Markham will be *snapped up.*' " She leaned forward toward Elizabeth, who was sitting opposite, and gazed at her face, which was looking wraithlike in the flickering light from the carriage lamp. "Have you been ill, my dear? Your face is thin, and you have shadows under your eyes."

"No, I have not been ill," replied Elizabeth, wondering if Mrs. Burlington could ever stop talking for at least five minutes. "It must have been the shock of the accident."

"Ah, yes. How *stoopid* of me. Do you know Rosamund, duchess of Dunster, well?"

"Not at all, Mrs. Burlington."

"A strange woman. One would not think Lord Charles came out of *that* stable, but you will see for yourself. Lady Jane, her daughter, Lord Charles's sister, is a gay little thing. She did not make her come out until a year after you, so no doubt you know her."

Elizabeth shook her head.

"We are very late in arriving, are we not? Perhaps they will all be abed."

There was a crunching sound as the wheels of the carriage moved from the smooth driveway to the graveled surface of the entrance court of the house.

"We are here. We are arrived. Wake up, Mr. Burlington," said Mrs. Burlington, giving her husband a jab in the ribs with her elbow.

Elizabeth's heart began to hammer against her ribs. She could not see much of Hatton

Court except that the building looked Elizabethan.

She was so tired that when she stood in the entrance hall beside the Burlingtons, the black-and-white tiled floor seemed to rise and fall beneath her feet.

A stately butler took Mr. Burlington's card and announced that the family and guests had retired to bed, but if they would care for some refreshment . . . ?

"Oh no," said Mrs. Burlington cheerfully as Elizabeth's stomach gave a hollow rumble. "We ate just an hour ago at a very good posting inn."

In a daze of fatigue and hunger, Elizabeth followed a grand housekeeper up the shallow steps of the central staircase. She was ushered into a very pretty bedroom decorated in blue-and-white. Blue-and-white willow-pattern paper ornamented the walls, and the bed hangings and curtains were of blue-and-white chintz.

A fire crackled on the hearth, and two housemaids set about unpacking her trunks under the supervision of a stern woman who turned out to be Mrs. Burlington's lady's maid, sent to attend to Miss Markham's comfort.

It was strange to have a lady's maid to brush her hair and to warm her nightgown at the fire, thought Elizabeth. If only she could get something to eat!

It was only after the lady's maid and the

housemaids had left that Elizabeth realized she was no longer the poor relation of Chuff House but Miss Elizabeth Markham of Mrs. Burlington's party. She could have ordered one of the maids to fetch her something to eat.

She eyed the long embroidered bell pull but then decided she had not the courage to bring herself too much to the notice of the servants.

She was so hungry she thought she would not sleep, but no sooner had her head touched the pillows than she plunged headlong into one of the deepest and most restful sleeps she had had for a long time.

It was the smell of toast and coffee, tea and bacon that woke her early.

The servant had not been in yet to draw the curtains and to help her dress, but Elizabeth decided she must go downstairs and find some breakfast as soon as possible.

She put on a pretty pink sprigged muslin gown. Her hands automatically began to braid her hair into those tight, hard braids until she realized she could wear her hair any way she liked. She twisted it into a knot on top of her head, allowing a few silver-gold curls to fall to her shoulders.

Elizabeth was too hungry to take in much of her surroundings or even to look out of the window. Food had become an obsession.

Lord Charles Lufford glanced over his morning paper and then raised it again like a shield. Interfering, shameless women! He had had enough of them the night before; he had hoped to be allowed to breakfast in peace since the ladies usually breakfasted in their rooms, but now it seemed he was to be ogled and simpered at once more.

He lowered his paper as he realized he would at least have to offer to serve the minx with something or other. She would probably leer at him, say she never ate anything more than dry toast, and would then prose on about the delicacy of her system.

He frowned quite horribly on Elizabeth Markham. He did not recognize her. He saw a thin, white-faced girl whose deep blue eyes seemed too large for her face. To his surprise, she was not looking at him. She was staring at the food left on his plate with single-minded intensity.

"Shy," he thought with a mental shrug. "That at least makes a change."

Elizabeth had recognized *him*, but for the moment, he was simply some piece of machinery that might serve her food if she pulled the right lever, and if he did not, then she had every intention of flouting convention by serving herself, although one was not supposed to do that if there were a gentleman present.

"May I offer you something, miss . . . ?"

"Yes," said Elizabeth bluntly. "I am very hungry."

He turned to the sideboard and began to

raise the silver lids of various covered dishes. "Let me see," he said. "We have kidneys, ham, kedgeree, cold pheasant, shrimps, oysters, eggs, toast, muffins . . ."

"Yes," said Miss Elizabeth Markham.

"*All* of it?"

"Yes," said Elizabeth fiercely, closing her eyes and wishing he would *hurry up.*

"I do not know if it will all go on one plate, ma'am," he said plaintively. "I shall have to furnish you with a series of plates."

She did not reply, merely sat there with her fists clenched tightly on her lap and her eyes closed as though praying for patience.

Lord Charles put two large rashers of ham, six grilled kidneys, and two eggs on a plate and put it down in front of Elizabeth. He replaced the covers on the dishes and returned to the table and took up his newspaper. Before he started reading, he glanced at Elizabeth and then stared. She was sitting over a perfectly empty plate, gazing at him with huge eyes, "like a dog waiting for its dinner," he thought.

He returned to the sideboard and piled a plate high with food and set it in front of her. She ate, not so rapidly this time, with steady concentration.

"May I help you to more?" he asked.

"Yes . . . please," said Elizabeth. "And beer, if you please."

He could feel his thin eyebrows climbing up his face and dragged them down.

Seeing that she was demolishing her third plate of food more slowly, he sat down, but this time he did not pick up the newspaper. It struck him that he had only ever seen such a ferocious appetite among the very poor. And what kind of young miss was it who drank beer with her breakfast? He did himself, but the only ladies he knew who drank beer were very old.

Elizabeth began to feel a comforting glow beginning to spread through her body. She smiled mistily at Lord Charles, who smiled cautiously back, seeing him not really as Lord Charles Lufford but as a provider of food.

"I do not believe we have met," he said. "I am Lufford."

"I know," said Elizabeth. "We have met. I am Elizabeth Markham."

He bit back a surprised exclamation. Elizabeth Markham! Her hair was still the same glorious color and her eyes the same sapphire blue, but she had a *wasted* look. Her arms were very thin, and her hands looked almost transparent. And yet she was not so very greatly changed physically. It was her manner that was so different. No wonder he had not recognized her. The Elizabeth he had known in London had seemed somehow older and had most certainly been bolder.

"Have you been ill?" he asked gently.

"No, not ill," said Elizabeth. "I was very hungry."

"I was sorry to hear of your parents' death.

Your uncle took you somewhere north, I believe."

"Yes, somewhere north."

"He is here?"

"No, I came with Mrs. Burlington."

"And what have you been doing since I saw you last, Miss Markham? Breaking more hearts?"

"No," said Elizabeth. "My uncle is concerned with the church. I do a great deal of parish work."

"Highly commendable. Does your uncle reside near here?"

Elizabeth dropped her eyes before his steady green gaze. The windows of the breakfast room were open, and the heavy smell of flowers and grass hung in the air.

"Excuse me, my lord," she said abruptly. "I am in need of some fresh air."

"Then allow me the pleasure of escorting you."

"No," she said harshly, and then, "no," in a quieter voice. "I would like to be by myself for a little."

He remained standing until she had left the room, and then he crossed to the window.

Elizabeth Markham walked sedately across the lawn in the sunshine, the thin muslin of her gown fluttering against her legs. She had gone some way and obviously thought she was out of sight of the house when she suddenly spread her arms and whirled about and then darted off toward the woods.

"How very odd," thought Lord Charles. He returned to his newspaper, but Elizabeth Markham's face seemed to rise between his eyes and the printed page. She was much altered. The death of her parents and the loss of her fortune must have been a hard blow. He remained frowning, thinking hard. He decided he was piqued. Elizabeth Markham was not the slightest bit interested in him, nor had she ever been.

Elizabeth finally sank down on a log in the middle of a glade in the wood. It was very quiet and still. The cathedral arch of the trees sent green-and-gold light down through the shifting leaves to dapple the glade.

Elizabeth felt a heady sensation of freedom. Her uncle would never think of looking for her here. After some moments the wonderful feeling began to fade. After the ball, the house party would begin to break up. The Burlingtons might ask her to stay with them, but they would expect a letter from her uncle. They would ask questions.

There was only one escape. Marriage. Somehow she must find some man among the members of the house party who would be prepared to marry her out of hand, someone who would not object to her background and lack of fortune, someone who would love her so much that he would be able to stand up to her uncle.

Elizabeth never thought of loving in return.

She now belonged to that large oppressed class of women — those who *had* to marry. In return, she would be a meek and modest wife, would bear children and run the household. No man should expect more. She thought briefly of Lord Charles. He made her feel uneasy. Had she not been so very hungry, she would have fled the breakfast room as soon as she saw him.

He had not changed. He had been as impeccably dressed as ever. He still had that overwhelming presence, that aura of command and masculinity that had made her feel so uncomfortable. His hair was still jet black and his eyes still that clear green, unmarred by even a fleck of hazel.

It was of no use to consider Lord Charles as a possible husband. That was reaching *too* high. What she needed was a modest young man, a member of the gentry like herself, with a comfortable income, not too high in the instep, and with a great deal of courage.

A cloud crossed the sun high above the arch of the trees. She gave a little shiver. It was time to return to the house, time to begin the husband hunt.

As she was approaching the mansion, she saw a young girl coming toward her. There was something familiar about that black, black hair and those green eyes.

"I don't know you," said the girl, coming up to Elizabeth. "Are you just arrived?"

"Last night," said Elizabeth. "I am Elizabeth Markham. I came with the Burlingtons."

"I am Jane Lufford," said the girl. This, then, must be Lord Charles's sister, thought Elizabeth. At first glance Lady Jane was very pretty. Her black hair was curled all over her head in artistic disarray, and her wide catlike green eyes were not shielded by heavy lids as her brother's were. She was wearing a morning gown of apple-green silk with many flounces, tucks, and gores. Elizabeth judged her to be some two years younger than herself.

"Do you want to marry Charles, my brother?" she suddenly heard Lady Jane ask.

"No," said Elizabeth, startled. "Should I?"

"Oh, everyone here wants to marry Charles, and it is so *boring*. They use me, you see, as a means of getting closer to Charles."

Lady Jane's face took on a brooding look that robbed it of beauty. Elizabeth noticed that her nose was long and sharp and that the translucent whiteness of her skin owed all to a liberal use of *blanc* and nothing to nature.

"It is all this frenzied race to get married that is so tedious," said Lady Jane, putting an arm about Elizabeth's waist and beginning to walk with her into the hall.

"Perhaps it is necessary that the ladies do become wed," volunteered Elizabeth cautiously.

"Why?" Lady Jane stopped abruptly and fixed Elizabeth with an unnerving green stare.

"Because . . . well, because perhaps they must."

"For money, do you mean? Tish, at least we do not have *that* sort of female here. We are all very rich."

"Even rich ladies sometimes crave a home of their own and . . . and children."

"Children. Pooh! I do not believe it. I shall not marry just to breed like some low country wench."

"But what would you do to occupy your time in the future years?"

"I would do as I do now," said Lady Jane severely. "I paint watercolors and sew, and I am an expert in the other ladylike accomplishments."

Now what was wrong with all that? wondered Elizabeth, fighting down a feeling of dislike. Had she not thought the same herself not so long ago? She had merely become unaccustomed to the ways of the ton.

"Are you not ever afraid that the Good Lord meant us to be a little more of use?" ventured Elizabeth.

"We are placed in our appointed stations at birth," said Lady Jane, "and to refuse to accept that fact is going against God's will."

Elizabeth reflected that Lady Jane and Julius Markham might find themselves very much in sympathy with each other should they ever meet. She had once, in the early days of her rebellion, asked her uncle if she would not be better employed taking food to some starving cottagers instead of reading them scripture, and Mr. Markham had pointed out that it was God's will that people should or should not starve.

Elizabeth looked about her, trying to find some change of subject. "Your house is very fine," she said.

Lady Jane brightened and regained her former prettiness. "I will take you on a tour if you wish," she said. "I love my home. It is finer than Blenheim, I think. It has more *character.*"

Hatton Court was a jumble of architectural styles on the outside. The main building was Tudor and suffered only slightly from having had a Palladian portico grafted onto its front. The east wing was Gothic, full of spires and statues in niches. The west wing was relatively modern, with bay windows, wrought-iron balconies, and cupolas.

Inside, centuries of different tastes and designs were jumbled together. The present duke had inherited his ancestors' trait of never throwing anything away. Squat Jacobean carved chairs growled at dainty Chinese Chippendale designs. Huge marble statues brought back from various grand tours shone whitely in the gloom of the large rooms. Portraits lined the walls of the hall and climbed up the stairs to march along the walls of the Long Gallery.

Lady Jane kept her arm about Elizabeth's waist. Elizabeth was torn between dislike of the girl's familiarity and pleasure at being able to display the friendship of the daughter of the house to anyone who might care to notice.

There were very few guests about. Lady Jane became more and more animated as she described the glories of the dukes of Dunster. The Luffords had gained the dukedom from Henry VIII and had managed to add to their fortune by changing their allegiance and politics at just the right time. They had never fought in any wars, which Jane seemed to think was very clever of them and mourned the fact that brother Charles had been *idiotish* enough to fight in the Peninsula against Napoleon's troops. "Although he is not the heir," said Lady Jane cheerfully, "so it really would not have mattered so very much had he been killed. My eldest brother, Harry, Marquess of Bennington, is the heir, and *he* is very careful of his person, I can assure you."

Hatton Court was a very large, very rambling mansion. Elizabeth was just beginning to feel that she could not bear to look at another portrait or examine another room when Jane announced abruptly that she was tired.

"Some of the ladies will have gathered in the drawing room. Have you met Mama?"

"I have not yet had a chance to pay my respects."

"I believe Mama to be in the South Drawing Room now," said Lady Jane.

Elizabeth experienced a sudden suffocating

wave of panic. The duchess of Dunster would ask questions, would realize that Miss Markham had not been staying with the Burlingtons. The lie about the wrecked carriage would come out, servants would be sent to search the countryside, and word would get to her uncle.

"Come along," said Jane with an impatient frown. "I am not accustomed to being kept waiting."

Elizabeth went to join her, and the two girls went down the stairs together toward the South Drawing Room.

Chapter Three

The South drawing room had a fine plaster ceiling, elaborate with strapwork and jeweling, and a frieze depicting various birds and beasts. Intricately carved Stuart chairs were lined up against one wall like a row of dowagers, while French Empire chairs took the floor like gilded and overpainted debutantes.

A saint was being bloodily massacred in a canvas over the fireplace, and the other oils about the room depicted tiny English aristocrats being dominated by enormous Italian ruins while they promenaded on various grand tours.

Rosamund, duchess of Dunster, was enthroned in a large carved chair beside the window. Her hair under her elaborate cap was white. She had a long thin face, so pale it was almost translucent. Her heavy-lidded eyes were of a pale, washed-out blue, and her long mouth was perpetually primped up in the middle through years of effort to reduce its size to the fashionable little rosebud that was considered *de rigueur.* She was wearing a morning dress that was so vandyked and flounced and layered that it seemed to ascend to her throat in a series of steps.

"Mama," said Lady Jane, "Miss Elizabeth

Markham is come to stay with us."

The duchess's pale eyes studied Elizabeth from head to foot. "I have no recollection of inviting Miss Markham," she said.

Elizabeth opened her mouth to give her explanation of having arrived with the Burlingtons, but Jane forestalled her by saying, "Well, you did, Mama, and Miss Markham is here. Miss Markham considers Hatton Court very fine."

"And so she should," said the duchess. "There is not a finer residence in the whole of England nor a more aristocratic family."

Her pale eyes regarded Elizabeth with a fixed stare. "We have kept our bloodline clean of commoners. There is no bar sinister in our coat of arms."

Elizabeth murmured something indistinct that she hoped might pass for approval. She found this pale, chilly, haughty duchess overwhelming and longed to escape. She felt sleepy, a sleepiness shot through with fear that if she stayed longer, the duchess might begin questioning her about her own residence.

The door opened, and Lord Charles and his friend Mr. Bertram Seymour walked into the room. Mr. Seymour had small neat features and a thick thatch of fair hair. From the apprehensive look he threw in the duchess's direction, Elizabeth knew she was not alone in fearing Lady Jane's mama.

She was introduced to Mr. Seymour by Lord

Charles, and just as she was making her curtsy, a party of young ladies headed by Sally Harper burst into the room. Sally did not see Elizabeth nor did the others. They surrounded Lord Charles, laughing and giggling and begging him to tell them which one of them would be honored with a place in his carriage when they went on a picnic that afternoon.

Lady Jane gave an impatient shrug and left the room. The duchess frowned with displeasure and picked up a book. Elizabeth found herself with Mr. Seymour outside the circle surrounding Lord Charles.

"Have you just arrived?" asked Mr. Seymour.

"Yes, last night," replied Elizabeth.

Mr. Seymour tugged at his stock, obviously trying to think of something to say. "Come far?" he asked after a few moments.

"Quite," said Elizabeth.

His face became quite pink with the effort of finding something else to say, so Elizabeth volunteered, "I took a little walk in the grounds earlier this morning. The weather is very fine."

"Isn't it? *Isn't it?*" said Mr. Seymour with enthusiasm. "We are very lucky to have such good weather so early in the year. The journey from London was pleasant, too."

He looked into Elizabeth's deep blue eyes and experienced a pleasant sort of drowning sensation. "I say," he blurted out, "we saw a most strange thing on the road. There is a town near here called Bramley."

"I have heard of it," said Elizabeth faintly.

"Well, as we were driving through, we saw this girl *escaping* from the window of a very tall house. Probably some servant. Anyway, she climbed up and over the roof. My heart was in my mouth, for I thought she would fall. Perhaps I should have reported the business to the nearest magistrate."

"I am glad you did not," said Elizabeth fervently. "I mean," she rushed on as he looked at her curiously, "it would seem a shame to get the girl into trouble when she had been brave enough to escape."

Mr. Seymour noticed the delicate color in Elizabeth's face that turned her lips to rose petals and felt his heart somersault. Behind him the bantering voices of the girls, begging Lord Charles to let them know which one of them he would escort to the picnic, rose and fell. He, Bertram Seymour, must find the courage to ask the beautiful Miss Markham to go with him before any of the other gentlemen arrived.

"I say, Miss Markham . . ." he began.

His voice was almost drowned out by Sally Harper's rather shrill voice saying, "Come, Lord Charles, you must not keep us in suspense. Which one of us is it to be?"

"Miss Markham," bleated Mr. Seymour desperately.

"Ladies," came Lord Charles's voice. "Give me a chance to speak. I was on the point of persuading my old friend Miss Markham to allow me to escort her when you dazzled my mind with your pretty pleas. Come, Miss Markham," he went on, leaving his circle of admirers to join her, "take pity on me."

He had a singularly sweet smile on his lips, but the smile did not reach his eyes. Elizabeth did not want to go with him. She knew too late that the pleasant and shy Mr. Seymour had been on the point of inviting her, and she would much rather go with him. But at that moment Her Grace put down her book and said loudly and clearly, "Most unsuitable, Charles."

Lord Charles kept his eyes fixed on Elizabeth, but he said, "Then you should not read such shocking literature, Mama. I trust you *are* referring to something you have just read?"

There was an embarrassed silence. "Yes, thank you," said Elizabeth, feeling that if she did not speak, Her Grace would start to elaborate on her remark.

The attention of the girls was now on Elizabeth. "Elizabeth Markham!" exclaimed Sally. "I would not have known you. You are so changed."

She introduced Elizabeth to the others, and a circle of eyes surveyed this new interloper, eyes of various colors that now all seemed to carry the same tinge of green.

"Where is your home now?" asked Sally, patting her brown curls and glancing at Elizabeth's silvery hair as if to remind herself that blond beauties were not fashionable.

"In this part of the countryside," said Elizabeth.

"Where precisely?" pursued Sally, her wits sharpened by jealousy.

"Quite near," said Elizabeth firmly. "At what time do we go on this picnic?"

"At two o'clock," said Sally. "But where exactly . . . ?"

"Then I must rest," said Elizabeth. She turned on her heel and almost ran from the room.

Elizabeth had no time to brood over the danger of Sally Harper when she was in the privacy of her bedroom. The most immediate and pressing matter was what to wear. Not only did she have just one hat, but she was also very short of necessary accessories such as reticules, handkerchiefs, jewelry, and shoes. She did not even have a parasol.

The hat she had worn the night before was a smart creation, but it was made of felt and not at all suitable for an outing on a sunny day. She could, of course, plead a headache and stay indoors, but how on earth would she ever catch a husband if she did that?

There was a scratching at the door, and Mrs. Burlington came in. "I just had to see that you were comfortable, Miss Markham. Have your trunks arrived?"

"Not yet," said Elizabeth, flushing and

wishing she did not have to tell so many lies. "Lord Charles has offered to take me to the picnic this afternoon, but I fear I have nothing suitable to wear."

"You *must* go," said Mrs. Burlington. "Lord Charles! Such a catch. The other ladies must be furious. I have a vastly fetching bonnet. Come to my room and let us see what we can find."

"You are very kind," said Elizabeth miserably. "Perhaps I should send home, except that most of my good clothes were among the ones that appear to be lost."

Mrs. Burlington put her large head on one side. "There's something about you, my dear Miss Markham, that leads me to think your uncle is quite strict. Some of these bishops affect to despise worldly matters and expect their daughters or nieces to become married through some divine miracle."

"He *is* very strict," faltered Elizabeth.

"And he will no doubt blame you for the accident to your carriage? I thought so. Men are always so. My Tom, the mildest of creatures, I assure you, dropped five hundred pounds at cards t'other day and snarled at me that it was *my* fault."

Lady Jane appeared at that moment in the doorway. "Ah," said Mrs. Burlington, swinging around to survey her, "you are of a size. My dear Lady Jane, here is Miss Markham, short of a few clothes because her trunks have gone missing. Now what can we do about it?"

"I hear Charles is to escort you on the picnic," said Jane, pinning Elizabeth with a steady green gaze.

"I think he was anxious to escape from his admirers," said Elizabeth, "and considered he would be less troubled by the companionship of someone he had known in London."

"Ah, yes," said Jane, her face lightening. "As to the problem of clothes, I have far too many and never wear the half of them. Wait here and I will send my lady's maid and the other servants to furnish you with the necessary."

Mrs. Burlington's fat face creased up in thought as Lady Jane left. "It seems to me," she said slowly, "as if our Lady Jane don't like brother Charles showing an interest in any of the ladies."

"It is not that," said Elizabeth cautiously. "She said something to the effect that she was tired of females seeking her company in order to ingratiate themselves with her brother."

"Well I don't know how she's ever going to think differently as long as the man remains unmarried. There isn't a lady from here to London who would not consider herself in Heaven if he dropped the handkerchief."

"Not I," said Elizabeth. "I find Lord Charles rather overwhelming."

"He is really very kind," said Mrs. Burlington. "Only think how he got rid of those dreadful servants for us. He had no reason to do that."

Elizabeth smiled. "Nonetheless," she said, "I think I shall give Lord Charles as wide a berth as possible. Too much interest in that gentleman is certainly not the way to my hostess's heart — or Lady Jane's for that matter."

"The only way to Her Grace's heart is through the first ten pages of *Burke's Peerage*," said Mrs. Burlington roundly. "*Very* high in the instep is Her Grace."

Lady Jane's maid and several chambermaids arrived at that moment bearing armfuls and armfuls of clothes and accessories, which they proceeded to put away in the drawers and wardrobe.

"And too much interest in Lord Charles, were I so disposed — which I am not — would cause Lady Jane and her mother to start to inquire too closely into my background," thought Elizabeth. Mr. Bertram Seymour, on the other hand, seemed a pleasant and decent young man. Elizabeth decided to concentrate on him. He seemed very shy, but she was sure that if his affections were seriously engaged, then he would stand up to her uncle and forgive her her unfashionable relations.

After Mrs. Burlington had left, Elizabeth spent a pleasurable time choosing something to wear with the help of Mrs. Burlington's lady's maid, Martha. At last she decided to wear a round dress of lilac muslin over a white cambric slip. It had a short cottage sleeve and a plain back. On her head she wore a provincial bonnet of moss straw with a band and full bow the color of the dress, terminating in a pendant end on the left side and finished with a corresponding tassel. Over her dress she put on a Sardinian mantle of French net.

Long limerick gloves were pulled on her arms and dainty little shoes of stamped kid put on her feet. In her diamond-shaped reticule, she carried only a small steel mirror and a vinaigrette. Martha looped a fan over one wrist and then handed her a very fine Pagoda-shaped parasol in lilac silk.

Elizabeth remembered to carry the parasol by the ferrule rather than by the handle, reflecting that some of these fashion dictates seemed designed to make life awkward. Not only was it *de rigueur* to carry one's parasol the wrong way up, but one's fan had to be carried by the tip rather than by the sticks. It was permissible only to wear it looped around the wrist, as she was now doing, when setting out on an outdoor expedition.

She surveyed herself cautiously in the glass, taking courage from the richly dressed young lady who stared back. As Martha bustled about behind her putting away the rejected gowns, Elizabeth suddenly realized with a feeling of panic that she had no money whatsoever to give the servants' vails at the end of her visit. That would be one more thing to confess to her future husband.

"Courage!" muttered Elizabeth to her reflection.

And, in her mind, the trumpets sounded for her as she squared her shoulders and marched downstairs to enter that dusty, noisy arena where the game of Finding a Suitable Husband is perpetually performed.

The day had settled down to a mellow golden haze of sunshine when she drove out with Lord Charles in his high perch phaeton. To her relief, he did not seem to expect her to make conversation, and she was free to forget about her troubles for the moment and enjoy the countryside.

The world of her uncle's house seemed miles away from this colorful scene as the line of carriages rolled down the drive under the verdant green of the new leaves. Out into the countryside they bowled, fields and orchards seeming to swim in the hazy golden light. Orange-tip butterflies danced over the meadows, and hoverflies hung motionless before the early flowers of the cow parsley. The first blossom was opening on the hawthorn, and the tall meadow buttercup was starring the fields with gold. Linnets were nesting in gorse bushes, the male twittering excitedly on a high spray, while the female went deep into the bush with grass and feathers. Across the placid surface of a dark brown weedy pond beside the road on

Elizabeth's left, a proud mallard led a bustling little party of ducklings.

Tears pricked at Elizabeth's eyes. It had been a hard and bitter two years: two years of humiliation and heartbreak. The scars went deep. It seemed to her, all in that moment, that she would carry those scars with her through the coming years. The ones on her back from her recent beating might fade, but there would always be that deep cutting terror, that shaking insecurity that one day she might be dragged back to the dark prison of Bramley: Bramley, which was so very near but where the sun never seemed to shine and the children never seemed to laugh. God, as described by her uncle, was a terrible old man in a long flowing beard and long flowing robes, rather like a choleric colonel watching, always watching, for ways in which to punish the sinner. Elizabeth thought bleakly that she would never be able to pray again. Tears began to roll down her face, and the sylvan setting vanished in a blur of saltwater.

"I am persuaded you have been very ill and are not yet recovered," said Lord Charles calmly, handing her a large handkerchief. "Perhaps it would be better if we returned. I think you would be better lying down resting in a darkened room."

Elizabeth sniffed valiantly and blew her nose. She would now dearly have loved to return to her room, but she might draw the unwelcome attentions — and curiosity — of the duchess down on her.

"I have had the influenza," she said, sighing a little as she spoke. One more lie on to the already tottering column of lies. "My illness has left me weaker than I thought."

"And yet you said you had *not* been ill."

"I always think of illness as something very grave . . . like . . . like cholera," said Elizabeth.

"Influenza is a very grave illness and many die from it," he said. "Let me take you home."

"No," said Elizabeth, straightening her spine. "I will do very well. The fresh air is good for me."

"As you will. I have not seen you since your last Season. I plan to be in London this Season. I hope I may have the pleasure of dancing with you at Almack's once more."

"I fear my London days are over," said Elizabeth quietly.

"Indeed? A great loss to society. Your uncle does not favor the London Season?"

"No, my lord."

"But there must be many beaux in your neighborhood pursuing you?"

"No, my lord. I am too busy with church matters."

"Poor Elizabeth," he smiled. "They have clipped your wings. You must marry in order to fly again."

"Perhaps." She turned her head away to look out over the countryside, hoping he would stop talking. His gaze was too penetrating, his elegance too intimidating, his social rank too daunting.

"Remember, Elizabeth Markham," he said, and she could feel his eyes on her averted face, "those who have never been in love do not know the pain it can inflict and are apt to treat lovers too casually."

Elizabeth bit her lip. The old Elizabeth would have laughed and said something light and flirtatious and assumed he was paying her a compliment and implying that his own heart was engaged, but the new Elizabeth did not know what to make of his remarks and finally assumed he was being censorious simply to make her feel ill at ease.

He said no more, however, for the rest of the short journey. The site for the picnic turned out to be a beauty spot, a small lake bordered on the far side by jutting slabs of rock topped with silver birches, shaggy grass, and wildflowers. On a small, grassy beach the servants were already unloading hampers and spreading cloths.

The ladies sank down on the rugs spread on the grass, the pastel shades of their muslin gowns splashing color against the silky green of the new grass.

Elizabeth was helped down. She did not intend to spend any more time with Lord Charles. The hunt was up! It was time to survey the gentlemen.

Sally Harper and her friends were laughing and chattering together, so Elizabeth went and sat in the shade of Mrs. Burlington, who was fanning herself vigorously.

"My dear Miss Markham," she exclaimed. "It is like high summer. What a fetching toilette. And how you have ruffled all our pigeons' feathers by driving here with Lord Charles."

Elizabeth felt herself relax. There was something so reassuring about Mrs. Burlington's bulk and placid temper. Mrs. Burlington went rattling on in her usual way, and Elizabeth answered her with faint murmurs while she surveyed the gentlemen. Apart from Lord Charles and his friend Mr. Bertram Seymour and Mr. Burlington, there was a squat, choleric man in old-fashioned knee breeches with the duchess — that must be the duke, thought Elizabeth — and two young exquisites, rouged and pomaded; and lastly, standing a little apart, a tall, slim young man with one of the most beautiful faces Elizabeth had ever seen. It was saved from effeminacy by the strength of his chin. His gold hair curled about a generous brow, and his eyes were deep brown, an odd and seductive contrast to his golden hair. He was carrying his hat, gloves, and riding crop in one hand. He wore leather breeches and top boots with a blue coat. The large brass buttons of the coat winked in the sun. His hands were very long and white.

"Who is that young man?" asked Elizabeth when Mrs. Burlington paused for breath.

"Which one?" asked Mrs. Burlington curiously. "The two Bond Street fribbles yonder are Jeremy Prescott and his brother, Harold. Their family has lands Durham way. Ah, the gentleman with the gold curls? That may be some relation of yours, Miss Markham. That is Mr. Derwent Pargeter — Derry to his friends. Now he is of the Shropshire Pargeters, and *his* father was some sort of far-removed cousin of your mother."

"How do you know all this?"

"I have much time on my hands during the winter, and I look up and make trees of every family."

"The only relation of whom I am aware," said Elizabeth, curiosity outweighing caution, "is my uncle Julius."

"The bishop? I had heard, of course, that he had taken orders, but I was not aware he had risen so high. Sophy, your mama, once told me that she and your father had scores of relatives with whom they had lost touch. Poor things. They were too busy enjoying themselves to visit or write."

The young ladies of the party had risen to their feet and had begun to walk about. Elizabeth saw that Lord Charles and Mr. Seymour were walking together toward the other side of the lake, deep in conversation.

"Go and talk to your young friends," said

Mrs. Burlington. "I know you young ladies would rather be chattering about beaux."

"I do not really know anyone very well," said Elizabeth. "I knew Miss Harper slightly when I was in London. But I may as well stretch my legs. Oh, I beg your pardon!"

Mrs. Burlington smiled comfortably and nodded her head. Elizabeth walked off, lecturing herself. She would never have dreamed of talking about "stretching her legs" in that free-and-easy sort of cant in her uncle's house, so why begin here, where it was definitely not the thing to say? She found Jeremy Prescott bowing before her.

He introduced himself and then his brother. Elizabeth curtsied, wondering why she felt so shy and tongue-tied. Would she never regain her lighthearted ease of manner? —

"I do enjoy these simple, peasant, alfresco meals," said Harold Prescott earnestly. "One becomes so jaded in the city."

Elizabeth took in the glory of the scene, the masses of servants, the hampers of delicious food and fine wine, the white cloths, and the small band of musicians who had just arrived and who were tuning up their instruments, and she could see nothing peasant or simple about it at all but forbore from saying so.

"It is very pleasant," she murmured, her eyes straying to Mr. Pargeter, who had walked forward and was hovering behind Harold's shoulder, obviously waiting for an introduction.

"I am lately come from London," went on Harold Prescott, "but, i' faith, I am sadly lacking in on-dits. Do you know any of the latest, Miss Markham?"

Elizabeth resolutely banished all the miseries and humiliations of the past two years from her mind. She laughed gaily, a charming laugh that carried across the small lake to where Lord Charles was walking with Mr. Seymour. "I am afraid my London days are over, Mr. Prescott. I am sadly provincial."

"By Jove," said Harold's brother, Jeremy. "One would need to be mad to consider *you* provincial, Miss Markham."

"Markham?" Mr. Pargeter moved forward to join them. "Now where have I heard that name before?"

Rather sulkily, Harold introduced him.

"Mrs. Burlington informs me that we are distantly related," said Elizabeth.

"That *is* news," exclaimed Mr. Pargeter, "but it gives me prior claim on your attention. Pray walk with me a little, Miss Markham, and we shall clamber through the branches of our family tree together."

"That's not fair," said Harold hotly. "I was here first." Half-angry, half-joking, Jeremy added his protests to those of his brother, while Elizabeth, the center of attention, laughed and blushed before she moved away on Mr. Pargeter's arm.

"Once a flirt always a flirt," said Lord Charles savagely.

"Eh?" said Mr. Seymour, startled. For his friend had been talking about horseflesh only a moment before.

"She always was a flirt," confided Sally to the other girls. "Elizabeth Markham does it quite deliberately, of course. She attracts every man to her side by her bold ways. Disgusting."

"What did Mrs. Burlington say?" Mr. Derry Pargeter was asking.

Elizabeth wrinkled her brow. "She said your father was some sort of far-removed cousin of my mother."

"Perhaps. I shall study the family Bible when I return home. How far did you have to travel to reach here, Miss Markham?"

"Not very far. Oh, look, those ducks. So pretty," said Elizabeth.

Mr. Pargeter's face was even more beautiful close up than it had appeared at a distance. His brown eyes had long, curling, girlish lashes, and his skin was tanned a light gold. He looked politely at the ducks and then said, "The ball is to be very grand. Most of the county will be attending, all the aristocracy and gentry. I plan to make my way south the morning after it. Or rather, that is what I had planned to do. I did not expect this circumstance to arise."

"What circumstance?"

"Why, your grace and beauty, Miss Markham."

"I am persuaded you are an incorrigible flirt, sir," said Elizabeth, not aware that several pairs of watching, angry eyes were blaming her for just that thing.

"Not I. Honest to a fault."

They had completed a small circle and were walking sedately back toward the rest of the picnic party as they talked. Lord Charles and Mr. Seymour had finished their walk and were rejoining the group. The brothers Prescott tit-tupped back into the pursuit of Elizabeth, the high heels of their boots stumbling over the springy turf.

"Pargeter's had enough of your time, 'pon rep," said Harold. "Now you must choose one of us to favor with your company, Miss Markham."

Elizabeth felt the old exhilaration at being the center of a ring of masculine attention. Mr. Seymour had now joined the men and was hovering, moving from foot to foot. Lord Charles stood a little apart, tall, harsh, and handsome, his green eyes cool, watchful, and cynical.

"I am embarrassed," laughed Elizabeth, "and so to save myself further embarrassment, it appears I must make a choice. And so . . . I choose you!"

She pointed her fan at Mr. Seymour, whose eyes lit up with pleasure. There were loud, mock groans of dismay as Elizabeth and Mr. Seymour walked away.

Lord Charles watched them go and cursed Elizabeth with all his heart. Only he knew how shy his friend Bertram really was and how

Bertram had been ruthlessly jilted by some callous flirt only a year ago. He was slowly recovering from his hurt. Now thoughtless, heedless Elizabeth was going to open up his wounds again — and pour salt in them, thought Lord Charles bitterly. Although she was still too thin, the fresh air had brought pink roses to Elizabeth's cheeks, and the rich clothes hid the frailty of her body.

He heard the rattle of carriage wheels. A country road ran along a ridge that overlooked the lake. On it was an open landau containing a clergyman and his wife and two antidotes who must be his daughters. The duchess of Dunster rose to her feet and raised her double eyeglass in the direction of the carriage. "Who are these people?" she demanded of her husband. "Send one of the servants to tell them to move on. I do not like to be stared at like a freak in Bartholomew Fair."

The duke muttered a few words to a footman and then despatched him.

Julius Markham and his family watched the approach of the livened footman.

"Oh, Papa!" squeaked Prudence. "Never say her grace has sent her servant to ask us to join her picnic!"

"That may well be," said Julius complacently. Although he professed to despise the frivolities of the aristocracy, it had come as a blow to his pride to find out that several of the gentry of Bramley and some of the local worthies had been invited to the ball. He had fully expected to receive an invitation himself, which he had assured himself and his God that he would refuse. But his pique had become great as the days had flown past and no invitation arrived.

The girls giggled and nudged one another as the footman approached. Patience took out a small telescope and put it to her eye. "Cold pheasant," she said. "And *ices*."

"Yes, my man," said Julius as the servant reached the landau. The footman's face was like wood. "His grace says for you to move on, sir," he said, "and begs to remind you, if by any chance you might be a gentleman, that it is vulgar to stare."

A dull, ugly red climbed up Julius's pale cheeks, while his wife and daughters bridled at the insult. "Tell his grace," said Julius awfully, "that we were merely pausing to admire the view. Say that Mr. Julius Markham sends his compliments and will pray for his grace's soul. Walk on," he snapped to his coachman.

Mr. Seymour wondered desperately what he could possibly have said to upset his ravishing companion. She was very tense and was staring fixedly into space.

Elizabeth had recognized her relatives. The footman returned. She was near enough to hear what he said.

"Gentleman presents his compliments and says he will pray for your grace's soul," said the footman.

"Jackanapes," grumbled the duke. "What's the feller's name?"

Elizabeth held her breath. If the footman said, 'Mr. Julius Markham,' she would immediately be questioned about her uncle the supposed bishop.

"Mr. Gules Meissen," said the footman.

The duke's face cleared. "Oh, a *foreigner.* That explains it."

Elizabeth let out a long sigh of relief, not yet knowing how near she had come to exposure; not knowing that had Patience turned her telescope on the guests instead of the food, she might have been discovered.

"I am sorry, Mr. Seymour," she said gaily. "What were you saying?"

"Nothing very important," he said, smiling with pleasure and relief. For one brief moment, he had thought the beautiful Miss Markham was about to faint.

Mr. Julius Markham returned home in a foul temper. He dreamt of the day when Nonconformist ministers such as himself would be the spiritual leaders of the country and even dukes would bow before them.

His temper was not improved when the maid told him there was some strange lawyer gentleman waiting to see him.

He had not yet discovered Elizabeth's absence, since his maid had told him before he set out that Miss Markham was sleeping and could not be roused. He had given orders to leave her to sleep, and the only bright spot on his horizon was the prospect of lecturing Elizabeth on the sin of sloth. Telling the maid, Perkins, to bring tea and cakes, Mr. Markham went to his study, where the lawyer was waiting for him.

A thin, elderly man rose to meet him. He introduced himself as Mr. Thomson and said he was dealing with the estate of Mr. Endicotte, Julius Markham's late uncle.

"Well, well, well," said Julius, visibly thawing. "I did not know poor Uncle Giles had departed this earth."

"He was a rather eccentric gentleman," said Mr. Thomson. "Mr. Endicotte was extremely fond of your brother, Mr. Peter Markham."

"Ah, yes, poor Peter."

"Mr. Endicotte left instructions that he did not want his relatives to be informed of his death until he was buried. He said he did not like any of them save one."

"Bless my soul!" A gratified flush spread over Mr. Markham's features. "I must say I never thought Uncle Giles cared for me particularly."

"I am afraid he did not, Mr. Markham."

"In that case . . ."

"It was Miss Elizabeth Markham, your niece."

"But he never set eyes on her."

"Yes, once, when she was little. Mr. Endicotte, as I have pointed out, was extremely fond of your late brother. In short, he has left his house and grounds and a tenth of his wealth to a local charity on the understanding that both house, grounds, and money will be used to establish an orphanage."

Julius's face went through amazing contortions. As a man of God, he could not protest against such a charitable bequest. But it was monstrous unfair!

"But the rest of the money?" he asked.

"That is to go to Miss Elizabeth Markham. It will come to you first with the instructions that you are to do all in your power to secure a suitable marriage for her. On that marriage, the money goes to her."

"How much?"

"Thirty thousand pounds."

"Thirty . . . !" Julius turned a grayish color. "And if she does not marry?"

"In the event of her not marrying, then you would continue to have the management of her money."

The door of the study opened, and the maid, Perkins, came in with the tea tray.

"Perkins!" said Julius harshly. "Go and fetch Miss Elizabeth immediately."

He helped his guest to tea and then sat back and rubbed his chalky hands thoughtfully. He had a clear picture of Elizabeth in her charity blacks, bowed and cowed. It would be a simple matter to keep the girl from marrying. Not that it wasn't for her own good, he assured his conscience. The money would be better put to enhancing his church and bringing more poor souls into the fold.

He roused himself to chat with his guest. They were just praising the exceptionally mild weather when a shriek rent the house from end to end.

Old Mr. Thomson sprang to his feet and sent his teacup rolling into the hearth.

Julius wrenched open the study door. Perkins came running down the stairs, her hand to her mouth.

"She's gone!" she screamed.

Mrs. Markham, Patience, and Prudence came crowding down the stairs behind the maid.

Julius darted forward and thrust them aside on his way upstairs. In Elizabeth's bedroom the uncovered mop lying on the bed bore mute witness to the trick she had played. He rounded on the maid, who had followed him up. "You told me this morning she was still asleep. Why did you not discover this until now?"

"The room was dark," said Perkins, beginning to sob. "I shouted and shouted, and when I didn't get no reply I decided miss was asleep."

Julius thought desperately. The girl must be found. She was now worth a fortune to him.

But first let him get rid of this lawyer.

He returned downstairs, brushing aside the eager questions from his wife and daughters.

Mr. Thomson was on his feet in the study. "I understand, Mr. Markham," he said, "that Miss

Markham has disappeared."

"Nonsense!" said Julius heartily. "It is merely some servant girl who has run away. Miss Markham is out on parish duties and will not be back until late."

"And yet you told the maid to *wake* Miss Markham," said the lawyer with a pointed look at the clock, which was just chiming the hour of five in the afternoon.

"That is very true," said Julius desperately. "Elizabeth said she had the Headache and meant to keep to her bed, but it seems she has recovered and is gone out."

"I can do nothing regarding the money until I see Miss Markham for myself," said the lawyer severely.

In vain did Julius cry out that he was a man of God and not in the way of having his word doubted.

At last the little old lawyer, obviously wearying of the tirade, said, "I have pressing business in the north and must travel on to Edinburgh. I will be returning through Bramley in about three weeks' time. If it please you, I will call then and satisfy myself as to Miss Markham's well-being."

"Yes, yes," said Julius eagerly. "Now, may I press you to stay and take supper with us?"

But Mr. Thomson had taken the reverend in dislike and was anxious to continue his journey.

Prudence came running up when the lawyer was being helped into his coat. "Did you find . . . ?" she began and jerked back with a yelp of anguish as her father stamped on her foot.

Glaring around at his womenfolk, his eyes signaling to them to keep quiet, Julius saw the lawyer on his way and then slammed the door and leaned his back against it.

"Find her," he said. "Turn out the whole town. Offer a reward.

"Bring her home and order bars for the window of her room."

Chapter Four

As the shadows were lengthening across the grass, Elizabeth stifled a great yawn. Once again she had eaten a great deal and felt immeasurably tired. She reflected that she had taken great steps in her quest for a husband. Perhaps too obvious steps, she thought wryly, looking across at the angry faces of the debutantes. Apart from Sally Harper and Frederica Spencer, the ones she recognized from her London days, there were two sisters, Josephine and Emily de Courcy, and a petulant blonde, Harriet Brown-fforbes. All had had one or two Seasons and were heading for the next but were hopeful of securing a husband before they got there. There was, after all, no other suitable career for a gently bred miss. But diminished as Elizabeth was in good looks, desperation gave her the edge on all of them, haunted as she was by the constant threat of being dragged back under her uncle's roof. Elizabeth had been aware of the duchess's pale, disapproving eye on her, but Her Grace's disapproval had slowly changed to indifference when it became all too clear that Miss Markham was not trying to ensnare Lord Charles. This might have been a sop to the other debutantes, but they could not help noticing how often Lord Charles's eyes followed Elizabeth as she moved here and there about the sylvan scene, with one of the other gentlemen dancing attendance on her.

The servants had packed everything away into the carriages and were setting out to Hatton Court. Elizabeth got reluctantly to her feet, unwilling to find herself alone with Lord Charles again on the journey back. The other gentlemen had been such undemanding company.

Mr. Seymour had been the most comfortable. He had a shy, pleasant manner and was able to talk intelligently on any amount of given subjects. Mr. Pargeter was tense and faintly acid in his humor but so handsome to look at that his most ordinary utterance seemed endowed with wit. The Prescott brothers were very much the Bond Street fribbles they appeared. Either of them would certainly make a most undemanding husband, since he would anguish more over the cut of a new coat than the household bills.

On the road home Lord Charles found to his irritation that Elizabeth Markham had fallen asleep with her head on his shoulder. Instead of rousing tender, protective feelings in him, her quiet tranquil sleep made him even more angry. This heartless flirt had spent all day setting one man against the other and yet held him, Lord Charles Lufford, of so little account that she had not made the slightest push to engage his attention. Lord Charles was not used to being ignored by anyone, particularly a young lady.

His was the last carriage to leave the picnic area. He let the reins drop and allowed the carriages in front to get well ahead and then gave his broad shoulders a massive heave so that Elizabeth's head was jolted. She came awake with a start.

"Are we nearly there?" she yawned. "I am so very tired."

"You remind me of a well-fed lioness who has devoured her prey and thinks nothing of the killed ones inside her stomach."

"What a very nasty thing to say!" exclaimed Elizabeth, now fully awake. She straightened her bonnet and glared at his profile.

"You deserve it," he rejoined equably. "You were an even more blatant flirt this afternoon than you ever were at Almack's."

"Fustian," said Elizabeth. "It is easy for a man to be censorious. He may marry when and where he may. A lady must wait to be asked."

"Strange," he mused. "I would not have thought you so desperate to marry. You have changed."

"I am not *desperate* to marry," said Elizabeth crossly. "You are merely piqued because I did not favor you with my attention."

This was so near the truth that he felt a great surge of rage. He slowed his team to a halt, and before she could guess what he was about, he clipped her about the waist and kissed her with such ferocity that the high perch of the phaeton dipped and swayed and the horses shied and whinnied.

Elizabeth drew back her fist to box his ears as soon as his mouth freed hers. She was burning and shaken and outraged. He caught her wrist and looked down into her stormy blue eyes.

"You do not seem to realize," said Elizabeth through her teeth, "that I have neither fortune nor fond mama to look out for my interests. I have no one in the world to protect me from the sort of insult I have just endured. If I had failed to attract the gentlemen's attentions this afternoon, I would not be labeled a flirt."

"I am sorry," he said with a blindingly sweet smile that Elizabeth found as shattering to her senses as his kiss had been. "I forgot your circumstances — and myself. It is too fine an evening to fight and quarrel. And you have been ill! I am persuaded of it. What a bear you must think me." He noticed there were purple shadows under her eyes and the wrist he still held felt thin and brittle under his grasp.

He released her wrist, picked up the reins, and looked at her, a glinting, mocking look. "Am I forgiven?"

"Yes," mumbled Elizabeth, "only don't *dare* to kiss me again."

"We'll see," he said with a laugh. "We'll see."

He gave the reins a light flick, and the carriage rolled forward.

Lord Charles, under his ease of manner, was thoroughly shocked at himself. He had stolen a good many kisses from innocent virgins when he was a much younger man, but never had he taken one in his arms before with such fury and passion. He decided that Elizabeth had cleverly and deliberately provoked such an assault. He had no intention of spending the rest of his days a bachelor, but he had no intention of proposing marriage to a green debutante. He had in mind a serene, mature woman of twenty-five or thereabouts who would ornament his table and grace his bed and who would produce a variety of heirs with clockwork regularity. Gently bred women did not have the same passions as men, nor were they expected to have them. There were women of the Fashionable Impure to quench any rampant lusts.

Elizabeth Markham aroused feelings in him that she should not be capable of arousing. Therefore it followed that Elizabeth Markham was not a lady under the skin. And having come to that seemingly logical conclusion, Lord Charles then wondered why he felt such a coxcomb.

He decided to give the girl a wide berth during the following days. He should surely not have to endure the sight of her for very long.

"Most of the guests will be leaving the morning after the ball, Miss Markham," he said. "Mrs. Burlington is certainly leaving then. I assume you will be going with her."

"When is the ball?" asked Elizabeth.

He looked surprised. "Wednesday."

And this was Monday! Elizabeth felt a sinking sensation in the pit of her stomach. Of *course* the ball was on Wednesday. But for some reason she had forgotten the date. So much work to do and so little time in which to do it. She had planned to have a tray in her room when they returned and then go to bed because she felt very tired. Now she would need to join the party for dinner and mark down one of these gentlemen and then get to work on him.

Her conscience gave an uneasy twinge at such ruthless behavior, but she fought down that still, small voice. Lack of success meant returning to Uncle Julius, and to live with Uncle Julius meant a short life of pain and drudgery. A party of workers walked wearily along the road, making their way home after their day's labors in the fields. The women looked picturesque in their lace bodices and kilted petticoats, the men strong and brown in their white smocks. Only now Elizabeth knew intimately how they lived, of their quarrels and drunkenness engendered by lack of money and lack of food. But they loved and laughed for all that and welcomed the birth of each child as a gift from Heaven. Red blood flowed in their veins, and they had great courage, a courage that anathema of society, the genteel poor relation, lacked, being neither fish nor fowl, neither worker nor aristocrat, shunned even by the middle class, regarded with contempt and suspicion by all. No, Elizabeth told herself fiercely, marriage is the only way I can survive, and I will reward my husband by trying to be a good wife.

"But if he loves you," mocked her conscience, "there is nothing you can do that will be sufficient in return."

"Better to love such as I," she told her conscience fiercely, "who will repay him with fidelity, than to find when love cools that the wife is straying elsewhere."

And so she calmed her conscience, unaware that Lord Charles was studying the expressions flitting across her face and wondering what thoughts could possibly be causing that deep intense look.

Lady Jane was waiting for Elizabeth when she reached her room. It appeared that Lady Jane had not gone on the picnic because she considered such outings "a bore" and was anxious, nonetheless, to be told the whole affair had been tedious in the extreme.

Elizabeth said it had been pleasant enough but very tiring, which Lady Jane seized on as proof that Elizabeth agreed with her idea of the futility of alfresco meals.

"I am afraid the other young ladies of the house party are quite disgusted with me," sighed Elizabeth, removing her bonnet. "They seem to consider me a flirt, but since *they* would not speak to me, I was practically *forced* into the company of the gentlemen."

"I suppose Charles was dancing about you as well," said Lady Jane sharply.

"Not he," said Elizabeth. "He was with his friend Mr. Seymour for most of the afternoon. Which was a pity. I find Mr. Seymour a most interesting young man."

"Oh." Lady Jane's face lightened, her fears that Elizabeth had been angling for her brother put to rest . . . as Elizabeth had meant them to be. "We must see if we can throw you together. I do not care for such manipulations for myself, but all ladies are not as I, and since I have a fondness for you, Elizabeth, I shall do what I can to help you to attach Mr. Seymour's affections to yourself."

"Thank you," said Elizabeth. "But I am not yet sure whether I wish to pursue Mr. Seymour seriously. I shall wait until tomorrow."

"Tomorrow we go to Barminster Fair," said Lady Jane. "I shall not go to that either, for it will involve a great deal of shrieking and demanding to see the freaks from Sally and her friends. Too tedious."

"But will you not be lonely here on your own?"

"Mama does not go either, so I shall keep her company. I am a very fond daughter. We are of such fine blood and high lineage that we sometimes find the company of lower people exhausting, although we do try so very hard to be sociable," said Lady Jane seriously. "You are fortunate being only of the gentry because *you* can feel a great deal more at home with quite common people like soldiers and vicars and the like. The sensitivity engendered by close contact with such people often causes Mama and me exquisite pain."

"How sad for you," said Elizabeth, fighting down a desire to giggle. "Does Lord Charles suffer the same type of anguish?"

"Undoubtedly, he must. He has the blood, you see. But he is a man, and men do not suffer from the same sensibility as women."

Lady Jane rose, shaking out her skirts. "Come and walk with me in the gardens, Miss Markham . . . Elizabeth? I may address you thus? I regret I have already done so without your permission. I desire fresh air."

Elizabeth was tired, and her head was swimming. She did not bother to give Lady Jane permission to use her Christian name, since Lady Jane's request had been merely a matter of form. She did not like to refuse the other girl's invitation, and Sally and her friends would not ask so many questions about her background if they saw she was in favor with the daughter of the house.

Also, Lady Jane had a rather gimlet eye and a way of making each request sound like a royal command.

Elizabeth nodded and said she would like a walk above all things, so Jane slipped a familiar arm about Elizabeth's waist as they left the room together.

The walk was exhausting since Lady Jane expected close attention to be paid to everything she said. Also, since it was the first time that day that Lady Jane had been out of doors, she was feeling fresh and rested and seemed prepared to go on walking around and through the gardens for hours.

At last the dressing bell sounded, and Elizabeth was free to retire back to her room to change for dinner.

Reminding herself fiercely that she was a guest in this mansion and not its resident poor relation, she rang the bell and demanded tea. Tea would perhaps revive her enough to face the rest of the evening, and then she would sink into that lovely soft bed and Lord Charles would most certainly have the opportunity to take his breakfast in solitary splendor in the morning. Elizabeth did not mean to quit her bed until noon.

The party was assembled in the South Drawing Room. Elizabeth asked for a glass of ratafia, that drink considered so suitable for the ladies and yet that had a kick like a mule. She managed to down two glasses while listening to Mrs. Burlington's chatter. Elizabeth was beginning to feel very warmly toward that comfortable lady who hardly ever asked awkward questions and was possessed of a great deal of kindness and sensibility.

Elizabeth was seated at dinner with the Prescott brothers on either side of her. Despite their fashionable airs and willowy figures, they were hearty trenchermen, and so she was not obliged to rack her brains too much to find things to say. Elizabeth began to feel mildly tipsy, and encouraged by the amount she had drunk, she essayed throwing a flirtatious glance down the table in the direction of Mr. Bertram Seymour. Unfortunately, he had leaned back in his chair just at that moment and the glance was intercepted by Lord Charles, who was leaning forward. He gave Elizabeth an outraged look followed by a haughty one as she began to giggle.

When it was at last time for the ladies to retire to the drawing room, the duchess entertained them all with a potted history of the dukes of Dunster, during which Sally Harper blotted her copybook by yawning horribly.

No sooner had the gentlemen joined them than the card tables were set up. Moneyless Elizabeth was bullied into making up a four with the Prescott brothers and Frederica Spencer. The game was whist, and Elizabeth, all too aware of her penniless state, played with a ferocity worthy of the most dedicated gamblers of Saint James's and nearly alienated the affections of the Prescott brothers, even Harold, who was her partner, by the grim and serious way in which she played.

They were playing only for shillings, but the other three were not aware that poor Elizabeth did not have even a shilling to lose. Lose she did not, but she was so numb with fatigue by the time the game was over that she promptly bid the company good night, to the disappointment of the gentlemen and the great relief of the ladies.

Before she went to bed, Elizabeth sat down at a little writing desk next to the window of her room and carefully wrote down the names of five men — Lord Charles, Jeremy and Harold Prescott, Derwent Pargeter, and Mr. Bertram Seymour. Then she wrote out their attractions or lack of them, the possibility of a proposal of marriage, and which one was likely to pop the question first. She did not waste much time over Lord Charles. "Arrogant and spoilt by too much attention," she wrote, "and if he is as insufferably proud as his mother and sister, then he would be impossible to live with. In short, a complete waste of time."

When she had almost finished, she wrote at the bottom, "On due consideration, Mr. Bertram Seymour seems the most likely candidate, and I have very little time in which to force the man to propose."

Satisfied, she undressed without ringing for the maid, blew out the candles, and plunged down into the deepest sleep she could ever remember.

Elizabeth woke very late. By the time she had dressed and made her way downstairs, most of the party had already set out for the fair, and she was lucky in that the Burlingtons were also among the last to leave and offered her a seat in their carriage.

Her heart sank when Mrs. Burlington said in her chatty way, "I think Frederica Spencer may be lucky in making a match before the Season. She was taken up by Mr. Bertram Seymour in his carriage, and he looked very well pleased with the arrangement, and Miss Frederica looked like the cat that had got the canary. Of course, *I* think Mr. Seymour is much too shy and naive a young gentleman for the likes of Miss Spencer, and Miss Spencer would not favor *him* were it not that she has had two Seasons and did not 'take.' "

Elizabeth was furious at her own folly in wasting so much time in front of the glass. But she had been so anxious to look her best. She was gradually losing the wasted look she had had when she arrived. Her cheeks were pink, and the shadows had faded from under her eyes. She was wearing a gown of Lady Jane's made from sky-blue jaconet muslin. It was of a very modern cut, the skirt being very scanty and the bosom rather low. The high waist had a girdle of rich white-figured ribbon. A little jacket of the same muslin was fastened to the waist of the gown by a white silk button. On her head she wore a bonnet of white willow shavings tied under her chin with a sky-blue ribbon. Elizabeth still did not find herself attractive in the least. She often assumed that it was her manner, her very flirtatiousness, that attracted the gentlemen. If she had thought herself beautiful, then she would not have considered that she needed to try so very hard.

It was only when they were on the outskirts of Barminster that Elizabeth suddenly asked how near they were to Bramley. "I believe only a few miles," said Mr. Burlington.

Elizabeth experienced a qualm of unease. Her uncle would never dream of attending anything so boisterous as a country fair. But what of the other townspeople of Bramley? She could only hope and pray that her fine clothes and fine company would be sufficient disguise.

The fair was a marvelous spectacle of color and noise, sideshows and booths. Elizabeth had a few shillings in her reticule that she had won at cards the evening before, and all at once, she felt like a child let out of the schoolroom. There were so many drolls and puppet shows it was difficult to decide which one to choose. One droll was called *The Tempest of the Distressed Lovers,* and the particulars of it were laid out in a playbill, which was thrust into Elizabeth's willing hand. In it were details of the story of the droll, which was about "The English hero and the Island princess, and the comical humours of the enchanted Scotsman, or Jockey and the three witches." Elizabeth read how the nobleman, after surprising adventures on the "Indian shore," married the princess and how "his faithful Scotsman fell in among witches, when between 'em is abundance of comical diversions. There in the tempest is Neptune and his Triton in his chariot drawn with sea horses and mermaids singing, with a variety of entertainment performed by the best masters; the particulars would be too tedious to be inserted here. *Vivat Rex.*"

When Elizabeth looked up from this fascinating playbill, it was to find that the others appeared to have vanished into the crowd. For the moment she was enjoying the heady atmosphere of the fair too much to worry about running after them or thinking of husband hunting.

Even the puppet shows offered elaborate stories — *Phaeton's Fall*, *The Story of the Chaste Susannah*, or *The History of Solomon and the Queen of Sheba*. But since the playbill for the latter promised Punch would add variety to the story by making "rude remarks about King Harry and the French" and "lay his leg upon the queen's lap in a very free manner," Elizabeth decided to spend her money on something a little more respectable.

At last she paid sixpence for an opera entitled *The Old Creation of the World* and entered the canvas tent and sat down beside a stout countrywoman right at the front. In later years Elizabeth was to attend many operas in London, but never would any of them give her the same intense thrill of excitement as this rustic performance in a dingy tent at a country fair. For two long dark years laughter and entertainment had been forbidden her, and so she enjoyed the performance more than anyone else there.

Noah's flood was represented by several fountains gushing colored water. Actors dressed as all the beasts of the field solemnly mounted up the rickety steps of the ark, two by two, while fowls of the air made of cardboard and tinsel sat among the trees as a gold cardboard sun slid down the edge of a painted rainbow. Scene followed scene with Dives rising out of hell and Lazarus lying in the bosom of Abraham.

As all this was going on, several figures were dancing jigs, sarabands, and country dances. Then came the comedians, two characters called Squire Punch and Sir John Spendall who made the audience rock with laughter, and then the whole show was "completed by an entertainment of singing and dancing with several naked swords by a child eight years of age."

Elizabeth clapped till her hands were sore. Then a man called loudly around the tent flap, "Is John Audley here?" — the traditional signal that there was a large enough audience waiting outside for the show to begin over again.

Elizabeth rose and began to make her way out slowly with the rest of the audience. It was then she realized she was attracting a certain amount of attention because of the richness of her clothes and because she did not have any servant with her. She resolved to find the rest of her party as soon as possible.

She had just emerged from the tent and was standing blinking in the sunlight when suddenly her arm was seized in a rough grasp. "There y'are," said a triumphant voice.

Elizabeth looked down into the unlovely features of Mrs. Battersby. For a split second she stared in terror, but then, drawing herself to her full height, which was only a few inches more than that of Mrs. Battersby, she said with a chill hauteur worthy of the duchess of Dunster, "Take your hand away. Release me this instant."

"But it's *you*, Miss Markham. There's an award for 'ee," gabbled Mrs. Battersby. "Reckernized you, all done up fine like you is and in among all them heathen."

A crowd was gathering.

"I do not know of whom you speak," said Elizabeth, standing very still and forcing herself not to struggle. "Now release my arm or I will send for the parish constable."

Elizabeth saw Lord Charles's tall figure heading in her direction. She simply must get rid of Mrs. Battersby!

Mrs. Battersby peered at Elizabeth's stony face and then released her arm. "I'm sorry, miss," she mumbled. "Made a mistake."

"Is anything the matter?" demanded Lord Charles, forcing his way through the ring of onlookers. "Pray God he doesn't call me by my name," thought Elizabeth. She took his arm, laughing lightly. " 'Tis nothing. Some poor woman has a touch of the sun."

To her relief he led her away. "It is your own fault, you know," said Lord Charles seriously. "You should not wander about without an escort. What delights of the fair can I show you? The two-headed cow or the pair of rattle-snakes?"

"I do not think I want to see any more," said Elizabeth. "Perhaps if you will escort me to Mrs. Burlington's carriage, I may rest there until everyone else is ready to return home." Elizabeth was now terrified of being recognized by anyone else.

"I can do better than that," he said. "I shall take you home myself."

"But do you not have to wait for one of the ladies?"

"I came by myself, so there is no fair charmer expecting to go home in my carriage. Come. You are quite white."

Still Elizabeth hesitated, the memory of his kiss seeming to still burn on her lips.

"You need have no fear," he said gently. "I shall not subject you to any excess of civility again."

Elizabeth walked beside him, her head down so that no one else would recognize her. She was very silent while they drove away from Barminster, and she did not raise her head until they were well clear of the town. Lord Charles was wondering what on earth had persuaded him to take the girl home when he had sworn only the other day to keep clear of her.

But she had looked so white and defenseless. She seemed to have made a remarkable recovery, he thought sourly, glancing at her sideways. She was sitting relaxed, her hands in her lap, gazing about the sunny countryside with evident pleasure.

"Did that woman frighten you?" he asked eventually.

Her hands clenched into fists in her lap.

"What woman?" she asked airily. "Oh, I remember. Yes. She did frighten me a little. She mumbled something, I know not what. Probably some gypsy trying to tell my fortune."

"She did not have the look of a gypsy."

"I want to forget her," said Elizabeth sharply. "Oh, do look!"

A little wood stood beside the road. Under the trees a mist of bluebells carpeted the ground.

He slowed his team to a halt and then backed them until the carriage was once more on a level with the wood.

"Would you like to pick some?"

Elizabeth shook her head. "They die too quickly. But I would like to get down for a little if I may."

He jumped down and tethered his horses to a tree and then helped her down. The sun struck down warmly on Elizabeth's back, and she removed her short jacket and carried it over her arm.

They walked a little way into the wood, and Lord Charles stood patiently while a rapt Elizabeth admired the flowers. Then his eyes narrowed as he looked at the low back of her gown. Across the smooth flesh above the gown was a network of scarlet weals. She turned and saw him staring and quickly put her jacket on again.

He helped her into the carriage, climbed up himself, and sat for a few moments holding the reins.

"Is anything the matter?" asked Elizabeth nervously.

He gave himself a little shake. "No, nothing," he said.

But he thought to himself that it certainly looked as if someone very recently had given Miss Markham a cruel and savage whipping.

"It *was* her. I swear it was," Mrs. Battersby was saying passionately as she stood in the study of Chuff House confronting Julius Markham. "When she pretended she didn't know me, well, I admit I was shaken, she looked that finely dressed a lady. I followed her when she walked off with the gentleman toward the carriages. Then as clear as day I heard him say, 'Are you comfortable, Miss Markham?' and her replies, 'Yes, my lord.' I asks about and found he's Lord Charles Lufford, the duke's son, so it stands to reason she's his doxy."

"Let me think," muttered Julius, walking up

and down and biting his knuckles. "No, that cannot be it," he said at last. "He would not keep her as mistress so near his parents' home. Mark my words, she met an old friend in the town and inveigled her way into the duke's household. I must think what to do. Thank you, Mrs. Battersby, you have done well and will be remembered in my prayers."

"The reward," said Mrs. Battersby, licking her lips. "There's a reward of five sovereigns."

"Come now, Mrs. Battersby, the reward was for anyone who managed to produce her."

"News of her, that's what you said," said Mrs. Battersby stubbornly.

Julius walked forward and held open the study door. "Good day to you, Mrs. Battersby," he said severely. "Lust after gold is a dreadful thing. You must cleanse your soul. I will, as I have already said, pray for you."

Mrs. Battersby left with tears of rage running down her cheeks. The more she thought of all the food five sovereigns could have bought, the more she cried. A year's worth of food! By the time she had reached her home, she had cried herself out. Her husband was sitting at the table. He was not drunk, although his breath smelled of beer. He fumbled in his pocket and shyly pushed a little painted fan across the table toward her.

"Bought this at fair," he mumbled.

Mrs. Battersby slowly picked up the fan and opened it, looking at the gaudy pictures.

"You're a good man," she whispered. "It's *him* that's bad and wicked, and he nearly made me like him."

As they approached Hatton Court up the long drive, Elizabeth saw that striped marquees were being erected on the lawns. She had wondered why there had not been more preparation in the house itself for the ball. She had not known it was to be held in the grounds. She had enjoyed the rest of the drive back. Lord Charles had talked easily and interestingly of his plans for his own estate in the south. It was very small, he said, but he was fortunate because younger sons of dukes were not usually so fortunate. His voice was deep and pleasant.

As he talked, Elizabeth studied him covertly from under the brim of her hat. His thick black hair curled under his beaver hat. His heavy eyelids veiled his eyes, and his long legs encased in skintight pantaloons and hessian boots showed a ripple of muscle when he braced his feet against the footboard. Although the afternoon was very hot, his starched cravat remained a miracle of white sculptured perfection: She could not forget that kiss. It made her hot just to think of it. Why had he kissed her? Had her stay at her uncle's reduced her to such a state that she had become the sort of woman with whom men instinctively feel they can take liberties?

As he spoke, Lord Charles found himself

wondering about the marks on Elizabeth's back. She must have done something terrible to have earned such a punishment. For some reason he found himself remembering that servant girl climbing over the roof. She had been a little like Elizabeth in shape and size. Had her master given her a beating, say she were caught?

But Elizabeth's relatives could not be so very strict, else they would not have allowed her to journey alone to this house party or to stay with someone as easygoing as Mrs. Burlington. The marks simply could not have come from a beating. She must have had a carriage accident.

All at once he found himself longing passionately for the end of Elizabeth's visit. She disturbed his well-ordered life, and worse than that, she made him ask questions about himself. It seemed to him as if he had never noticed before his mother's obsession with her high degree or his little sister's willingness to share in that obsession. Now he wondered whether he were equally guilty. He had never thought for one moment that he would ever consider marrying someone who was not his equal in rank and lineage. He had felt he owed it to his family name.

Yes, he would be glad to see the last of Elizabeth Markham and her changes of April mood, one moment laughing and gay and the next clouded in brooding loneliness. All he could do was take care of his friend Bertram and make sure he was not hurt by her wiles and deny that still, small voice in his head that was trying to warn him that this frail debutante was quite capable of inflicting hurt on Lord Charles Lufford himself.

Chapter Five

The day of the ball. Elizabeth did not have any opportunity to carry out her marriage plans. The gentlemen had all gone off to see a prize-fight. The mansion was alive with bustling servants, many of whom had been hired specially for the great day.

The day was warm — too warm. A false tropical summer in spring. Gallipots sent their scent of vinegar and sugar into the hot air of the elaborate, cluttered rooms, attracting sleepy flies. Curtains were drawn and blinds pulled down to keep out the heat, but the heat was already *in,* still and suffocating. Lady Jane said Mama had been told that there might be a mighty storm and had been advised to move the ball indoors, instead of holding the event in the marquees on the lawns but had, of course, refused, since God in His wisdom would not bring down a storm on the illustrious head of the duke of Dunster. After all, there wasn't a cloud in the sky.

But there was a thin veiling that turned the sun brassy and the sky to grayish blue.

There was a heavy, waiting feeling in the air that strung out Elizabeth's nerves to their fullest. Her whole dream of finding some gentleman in the house party prepared to marry her on such short acquaintance seemed mad and desperate. She had spent too much of the little time there was with Lord Charles. Just as much as she did not really belong in her uncle's house, so she felt an equal stranger at Hatton Court.

The busy little French clock on the mantel in her room chattered away, eating up the minutes and hours. Elizabeth was not used to being idle anymore. She had repaired a small tear in the gauze of her ball gown and had tried arranging her hair in various styles, but the very closeness of the air made even a little effort exhausting.

Perhaps life somewhere between the magnificence of the Dunsters and the poverty of, say, the Battersbys might be comfortable. A style of living where one might have to take on some of the duties allocated in a higher stratum to servants. Perhaps the life of a farmer's wife or the wife of a small tradesman was more full, taken up with the many chores of housewifery, although of late there had been many complaints that due to the excessive cost of wheat, the farmers and their wives had become so grand it was hard to tell them apart from the lords and ladies.

Elizabeth went downstairs and wandered into the grounds, feeling even more useless and idle among the bustle of the servants. The ball was to be held in one marquee and various types of refreshments in several others. More guests had arrived, middle-aged couples with children. No suitable, marriageable men.

As much of the ball as possible must be spent in the company of Mr. Seymour, decided Elizabeth. A Mr. Seymour suitably enslaved might listen to the true tale of her predicament. Her conscience gave a sudden fierce jab, but she thought of Julius Markham and his household, and she fought it down.

There were the Prescott brothers, of course, and Mr. Pargeter. Mr. Pargeter was very handsome, but Lord Charles's rather harsh, very masculine good looks seemed to make Mr. Pargeter's beauty appear somewhat too feminine.

Lady Jane materialized at Elizabeth's elbow. "How primitive some of these servants are," she complained. "They are convinced this odd weather is caused by Napoleon, that he has employed witches to cast spells for him and bake England as brown as the Sahara."

"The weather is very odd indeed," said Elizabeth. "Why, I have known it to snow at this time of year. The Season is only just begun."

"Yes," yawned Lady Jane, "and we are to travel to the townhouse after the ball — or a few days after it, rather. Dear Almack's! I pine to see it again."

"I never would have imagined you pining to go to Almack's," said Elizabeth, who had pictured Lady Jane and her mother as being constantly at Hatton Court, shuddering over contact with the lower orders and studying the family tree.

"Almack's Assembly Rooms," said Jane primly, "are all that is nice. The Italian Opera also. The committee makes sure that vulgar persons are not admitted so one can feel free to enjoy both without one's nerves being scratched by common language and Cheapside manners."

"I never thought of either of those places as being anything very special," thought Elizabeth. They were simply places one went to during the Season.

But she said aloud, "When are the gentlemen expected to return?"

"Ah, pining for your Mr. Seymour," said Lady Jane indulgently. "They will not be long. Charles knows he is expected to be on hand to greet the guests. There are some quite low people coming from Bramley. Papa believes in maintaining good relations with the worthies of the town. Is anything the matter, dear Elizabeth? You are become quite white."

"It is nothing," said Elizabeth. "By low people, do you mean people like Nonconformist ministers?"

"God forbid," said Jane piously. "Papa does have to draw the line somewhere."

Elizabeth let out a little sigh of relief.

A rumble of carriages from the driveway heralded the return of the gentlemen. The Prescott brothers looked well to go, and Harold was brandishing his whip and noisily singing one of those songs that seemed to be composed mostly of tollroll diddle-dols.

Mr. Pargeter said something to Lord Charles, who threw back his head and laughed. They all, even the quiet Mr. Seymour, were enclosed in a contented world of masculinity. Elizabeth began to experience something like stage fright.

Then she heard Jane say, "Oh, dear," in a quiet little voice, all her normal arrogance gone. Behind the gentlemen's carriages came an elegant traveling coach with a crest on the panels.

"Who is it?" asked Elizabeth.

"Lady Herne."

"I have not heard of her."

"She is a widow. Very dashing and very fond of Charles."

Elizabeth should have been grateful that Lady Herne was interested in the one gentleman she herself had considered unsuitable and wondered at her own sudden feeling of depression.

"And does Lord Charles show interest in this Lady Herne?"

"What gentleman would not?" said Jane gloomily. "Lady Herne is a diamond of the first water, and the gentlemen are not deterred by her common origins."

"But she is a lady. . . ."

"By marriage. Her parents are cits."

Despite a certain feeling of sympathy for Lady Herne, Elizabeth could not help feeling dismayed. Although she still did not think

much of her own appearance, she had, para-
doxically, not expected much in the way of ri-
valry.

"Your mama must think well of her," ventured Elizabeth, "else she would not have been
invited."

"Mama did *not* invite her. She has arrived
thus before. Always there is some pretty excuse.
. . . The wheel of her carriage broke. . . . She
just happened to be in the vicinity, and so on.

"Papa, unfortunately, always welcomes her.
She has been abroad until last year, and she has
been pursuing Charles ruthlessly, although he
seems unaware of the fact."

Elizabeth thought that Lord Charles, who
seemed remarkably alert on all suits, probably
knew very well that the dashing widow was attracted to him.

"If only Charles would not . . . *indulge* her
so," said Jane. "Dear me, this heat is frightful.
Although the servants still seem to be working
hard. Of course the northerner is much supe-
rior to the southerner, who is more torpid, because of the better climate."

Elizabeth contemplated pointing out that
these particular ones knew better than to slack
off for a moment under the hard eye of Her
Grace's butler. Being in service in a large house
meant guaranteed clothes and food. Dismissal
without a reference meant returning to the
mills, to cold houses, mouldy bread, lack of
bedding, and insufficient clothing. But she was

perfectly aware that Lady Jane would consider her knowledge of the conditions of the poor ungenteel, to say the least.

The footman over there was obviously in love with that pretty housemaid who was handing him up lanterns to string between the trees. What was their future? They could not marry, because then they would lose their jobs.

"It is late," said Lady Jane, breaking into Elizabeth's thoughts. "The dressing bell will sound soon."

Side by side, the two girls walked toward the house, each immersed in her own thoughts. Lady Jane was obviously still fretting over that peril to the family tree, Lady Herne, seeing her as a type of malignant and gorgeously colored caterpillar, all set to gnaw the succulent and aristocratic leaves of the Dunster family tree.

Elizabeth felt her stage fright mounting. What would tonight bring? Oh, if only her dear mother and father were alive, if only she had a home, so that she might enjoy this glittering event without having to plot and plan like an adventuress!

Elizabeth allowed herself the rare luxury of a full bath. Cleanliness was not considered next to godliness in Julius Markham's household. And since Elizabeth had to carry her own bath upstairs and then laboriously fill it up with jugs of water and then empty it afterward by the same slow process, she usually had to be content with taking a sponge bath, standing in a basin. Things were different at Hatton Court, where there was a whole army of servants to carry both bath and water up the stairs.

But no sooner had she toweled herself dry than she began to feel hot and sticky again. She dressed herself, having refused the offer of Mrs. Burlington's lady's maid for that operation so that the weals on her back from her uncle's whipping would not be seen and reported. There did not seem to be a breath of air in the room. She felt desolate and near to tears. For a moment she almost wished she had been set upon by some footpad on her long journey to Hatton Court and that she might even now be lying lifeless in the ditch, far removed from loneliness, fear of the future, terror of her uncle, the awful prospect of destitution if she did not find a husband.

She pulled back the curtains, which had been drawn against the sun, opened the window, and leaned out. The air outside was as thick and hot as it was inside the room. But the fairy lanterns glittered among the trees, and snatches of music from the band of musicians who were rehearsing inside the marquee floated up through the quiet air.

"I am Elizabeth Markham," she told herself fiercely. "I am a debutante and a guest in this house. If I do not set out to simply enjoy this evening, then I shall possibly waste the only chance I shall ever have of attending a great ball."

She turned from the window as Mrs. Burlington's lady's maid entered and composed herself to enjoy the expert finishing touches of a first-class lady's maid.

By the time she made her way downstairs, she was well satisfied with her looks. The gown of gold tissue whispered about her feet. Her hair had been elaborately curled and pomaded so that it shone like the whitest of gold.

She entered the drawing room, and the very first person she saw was Lady Lydia Herne. Although she had never met her, Elizabeth was immediately sure that the vision holding forth to a circle of enraptured men must be she. She had very black glossy hair cut daringly short and curled all over her head. She had very full, liquid brown eyes, a short straight nose, and a tiny mouth. In short, she was the perfect example of a society beauty. Perhaps the only fault to be found with her appearance was in her skimpy white muslin gown, which had been damped to reveal the full curves of her figure. Lady Herne was in her late twenties, too mature an age to wear white muslin. A collar of pearls emphasized the whiteness of her neck and arms. But her great charm was in her complete and absolute self-assurance. Every movement was seductive and well rehearsed, from the turn of her head to the way she raised one long hand to her bosom as if to draw attention to its perfection.

Lord Charles was standing a little away from

her admirers, looking amused. He was magnificent in evening dress, the stark black and white of his clothes flattering the whiteness of his handsome face and the blackness of his hair. One large, flawless emerald in his cravat complemented the green fire of his eyes under their heavy lids.

For the first time Elizabeth found herself welcomed by the other girls in the group — Sally Harper, Frederica Spencer, Josephine and Emily de Courcy, and Harriet Brown-fforbes. There were other ladies in the party, but they were either too old or too young to enter the matrimonial stakes. A great number of people were traveling to Hatton Court to arrive in time for the ball, but this augmented house party was the real battlefield.

"Is she not disgusting?" whispered Sally, waving her chicken-skin fan in the direction of Lady Herne. "Such blatant, bold manners. The gentlemen will take her in dislike very soon."

"I don't know how the dear duchess can tolerate her," said Harriet petulantly.

"Perhaps the dear duke is just as enamored of her as the other gentlemen," said Frederica nastily.

Elizabeth moved away and went to sit beside Mrs. Burlington. That lady gave a fat chuckle. "Escaping from all those ruffled feathers?" she asked.

"Lady Herne is very handsome," volunteered Elizabeth.

"Ah, she's set her cap at Lord Charles, and the duchess fears she means to wed him. But that ladybird does not care whether 'tis marriage or the other thing."

"Mrs. Burlington!"

"I only speak the truth. Lady Herne has been back in England but one year and already she has a certain reputation."

Lady Herne looked across the room and saw Elizabeth's wide wondering gaze, and taking it for one of admiration, she glided toward her, her court of admirers following sheepishly behind. Lord Charles remained, leaning against the mantel and looking amused, as if watching a comedy.

Flushing slightly, Mrs. Burlington made the introductions. "I am looking forward to the ball," said Lady Herne, fanning herself languidly. "But this heat! Let us hope we have some dashing nabob present. Such heat would delight him. Do you travel from London, Miss Markham?"

Elizabeth hesitated. To say that she arrived with Mrs. Burlington would not exactly be the truth, and Mrs. Burlington would certainly be surprised at the absence of description of the overturned carriage.

But her hesitation had been long enough for Lady Herne to lose interest in her. She turned with a laughing remark to Mr. Seymour, saw Lord Charles was still across the room, and began to undulate slowly in that direction.

To Elizabeth's discomfiture she became aware that her gallants of the picnic were avoiding her. Even when she rose and joined the other girls who were in turn joined by the Prescott brothers, she noticed that both Harold and Jeremy would never look her straight in the face. Their eyes slid off her.

Puzzled and alarmed, she began to feel dowdy. She grew quieter and quieter and found she could not join in the conversation.

By the time the laughing and jostling guests moved out to join the huge throng of new arrivals in the temporary ballroom in the garden, she was feeling so low in spirits she only longed for the hot evening to be over so that she could creep to her bed.

It was only when she was surrounded immediately by new gallants and once more the adoring center of attention that her flagging spirits began to rise, and it was some time before she realized that although she was an enormous success with these newcomers, she was being studiously avoided by the gentlemen of the house party.

The marquee that housed the ballroom was draped with crimson-and-gold silk, like an oriental tent. Great banks of hothouse flowers sent out a sweet, heady perfume that mingled with the scent of musk from the guests. Jewels blazed in the light of hundreds of candles. Some of the wives of the provincial worthies were barely concealing their shock at the near nudity of some of the highborn ladies. Despite the intense heat, Lady Herne danced gracefully, although she was not asked to dance by Lord Charles, Elizabeth noticed.

She herself had just finished promenading after an exhausting set of country dances with a young officer when Mr. Seymour approached her and begged the honor of the next dance.

Pleased and gratified, Elizabeth gladly accepted, beginning to think she had imagined the earlier coldness of the male members of the house party. When they were walking about after the dance, she turned the full battery of her charm on Mr. Seymour, who gazed at her with wide enraptured eyes like a child at Christmas. Elizabeth caught a flash of green dislike from Lord Charles and flirted even more.

"It is so hot," sighed Elizabeth. "I would like some refreshment."

"Allow me to escort you to the other tent," said Mr. Seymour eagerly.

Well aware of Lord Charles's eyes boring into her back, Elizabeth allowed Mr. Seymour to lead her outside and along the short walk that led to the refreshment tent. Mr. Seymour stopped suddenly and turned to face her.

"Miss Markham," he said in a low voice, "I consider you a pearl beyond price. I must admit, I was startled at what Charles said. . . ." He broke off in confusion.

"And what did Lord Charles say?" demanded

Elizabeth in an icy little voice.

In the light of the lanterns, it was possible for Elizabeth to see that Mr. Seymour was blushing miserably.

"You must tell me now," she urged. "I could not help but notice a certain coldness toward me from the gentlemen this evening."

"I think it was only a joke, only a joke," said Mr. Seymour wretchedly. "We were celebrating in an inn after the prizefight and, well, Harold Prescott gave the toast to Miss Markham. Charles refused to raise his glass. He said you were an expert breaker of hearts and making a game of us all. But now I see that it must have been his way of funning. He has an odd wit at times."

"Very odd," said Elizabeth, barely able to contain her fury. Lord Charles had not seen fit to warn anyone against Lady Herne, she who dressed like a courtesan and had not even been invited. In her fury, Elizabeth quite forgot that she had not been invited herself.

"Oh, my wicked tongue," said Mr. Seymour. "It does run away with me. Please do not be angry with me, Miss Markham."

"I am not angry with *you,*" said Elizabeth truthfully. "Let us walk on."

But when they were both seated in the refreshment tent with glasses of champagne, Elizabeth found she could not carry on her lighthearted flirting.

Hard as she tried, rage at Lord Charles continued to consume her. And so it was that when that gentleman himself came to join them, it was to find Elizabeth all heaving bosom and flashing eyes and Mr. Seymour downcast and guilty.

"It is a fine night, Lord Charles," said Elizabeth through her teeth. "I would be grateful if you could spare me a few moments of your time."

"I told Miss Markham what you said to us all," muttered Mr. Seymour, looking wretched.

Lord Charles's black brows snapped together. "I have a great many guests to attend to, Miss Markham," he said coldly. "Is it important?"

"Yes."

"Very well. Apologies, Bertram. I shall return Miss Markham to you in as short a time as possible."

Elizabeth controlled herself until they were out in the gardens and a little way from the marquees.

She swung round to face him as he came to a halt a little behind her. "How dare you," she began.

"Miss Markham," he interrupted wearily, "I am sure you yourself have at times made remarks about someone, at some time said something in jest."

"Never!"

"Indeed! It came to my ears some time ago that you had said to a certain Miss Darcy that my heart belonged soley to my tailor."

"That *was* a jest. I am persuaded you believed what you said when you warned the gentlemen I was a flirt."

"But that was something I had already told you direct."

"I demand an apology," said Elizabeth stiffly.

"My apologies, ma'am."

A long drumroll of thunder came from the high moors. A gust of warm wind sent the lanterns dancing, throwing Lord Charles's face into light and shadow.

All at once Elizabeth wanted to lean on him, to tell him of all her fears and insecurity. Perhaps it was a trick of the dancing, swaying lights, but his eyes looked kind and somewhat troubled as they gazed at her.

"Tell me," he said softly.

"Tell you what, my lord?" asked Elizabeth.

"Tell me why the beautiful Miss Markham, the belle of the London Season, should now be thinner. Why she is flirting outrageously, almost as if to disguise something frightened and harried and hunted underneath."

Elizabeth played with the sticks of her fan. She was almost on the point of unburdening herself when, with one mighty crack, the heavens above split open and jagged forks of lightning stabbed their reflections across the blank panes of the great mansion.

She let out a little yelp of alarm and threw herself into Lord Charles's arms.

He had sworn to himself that he would never kiss her again, but when he felt her pliant body in his arms, he was overcome by a bittersweet mixture of tenderness and passion. He murmured something unintelligible and bent his mouth to hers.

Elizabeth found herself racked by so many different emotions as his mouth pressed down on her own that tears started to her eyes and mingled with the huge warm drops of rain that were beginning to fall.

Then she found herself lost in a world of feeling and passion such as she had never known before.

The wind howled and shrieked in a growing frenzy, and the rain increased to a driving downpour. There were cries of alarm from the marquees as the thunder bellowed and roared. The ropes holding the tents strained and began to snap.

"Quickly, into the house," yelled a man's voice, and the guests came charging out, stumbling and falling in their panic to reach shelter, while a little way from the scrambling throng stood Elizabeth Markham and Lord Charles Lufford, locked in each others arms.

Like some huge live thing, the marquee that had housed the ballroom was whipped away, flying toward the woods like some gigantic bat, carrying with it a train of torn pieces of silk and swirling, dancing hothouse flowers.

Lord Charles freed Elizabeth's mouth and

looked down at her in a kind of wonder.

Elizabeth came back to earth with a bump. She was standing in the middle of a whirling, screaming storm, soaked to the skin, and demonstrating to anyone who cared to look, her complete and utter lack of morals. She had been only dimly aware of the fleeing guests.

It hit her with the force of the storm that all her hopes of marriage were gone. Lord Charles would not marry her — she was sure he considered her too far beneath him in rank for that — and no other gentleman would now even think of it since the blinding flashes of lightning must have lit up her embrace as if she were onstage.

"Elizabeth," said Lord Charles, his voice husky and strange.

She gave a little gulp, pushed his arms away, and ran headlong through the rain toward the house.

Elizabeth's dreams and hopes of escape lay in ruins. She scurried to her room as fast as she could, locked the door, undressed and dived into bed, pulling the covers over head, willing herself to sleep, willing herself to forget that the morning would mean facing accusing eyes.

Before she drifted off to sleep, she suddenly thought with alarm, "How very, *very* angry Jane is going to be, and yet she will forgive me, as she would forgive any woman who did *not* marry her precious brother."

Perhaps because of her very determination to

escape reality, Elizabeth slept long and late. She was awakened with the summons that Her Grace wished to see her immediately.

Elizabeth dressed quickly in a muslin gown of pale blue, with long darker blue silk ribbons tied round its high waist. It had three deep flounces, and the length was cut fashionably short to expose most of her ankle.

As she made her way downstairs, a great deal of her fright began to leave her. The duchess could not possibly mean to berate her in front of Lord Charles, in front of the other guests.

Elizabeth pushed open the double doors of the drawing room and then stood stock still.

The original members of the house party and the duke and duchess of Dunster, together with Lord Charles and Lady Jane, stood about in various attitudes of disdain.

And the objects of their disdain stood firmly in the middle of the duchess's Chinese carpet, staring about them with angry, defiant eyes.

They were Julius Markham, his wife, and their two daughters, Patience and Prudence.

Chapter Six

The game was up!

It was almost a relief in a horrible kind of way.

Outside the long windows watery sunlight shone on the sodden wreckage of the lawns. One lantern, brave survivor of the ball, swung jauntily to and fro in a stiff breeze.

Julius Markham was the first to break the dreadful silence in the drawing room.

"Wretch!" he said.

"Thief!" cried Patience and Prudence in unison.

"Doxy," grated Mrs. Markham.

Her white face even whiter with distaste, the duchess of Dunster made a languid beckoning motion with her hand. "Step forward, Miss Markham," she said. "These persons claim to be your relatives and say you escaped from your home."

"If it was her home," put in Lady Jane, "then why do they say she *escaped* from it. One only escapes from prison."

"Elizabeth is my late brother's daughter," said Julius Markham. "I have struggled for two years now to eradicate the devil that is within her. I can only mourn, Your Grace, that I have set such a devil loose in your home."

"Oh, I say," protested Mr. Seymour weakly.

"I really do not understand all this," said the duchess. "Mrs. Burlington, Miss Markham is of *your* party."

Mrs. Burlington looked worried. "I found the poor thing sitting in the grass outside the West Lodge when I arrived," she said. "Miss Markham told me that she had had an accident in her carriage and that she had left her servants and walked on ahead on foot. I declared her to be of our party because we arrived so late and it seemed cruel to have poor little Miss Markham having to give a lot of explanations. I thought, of course, that she had told Your Grace about the mishap later and that your servants must have already been searching the countryside for the wreck of her carriage. I confess after that I more or less forgot about the whole thing. Lady Jane graciously lent Miss Markham some clothes and so . . . and so . . ."

Her voice trailed away.

"So she has deceived you all," said Julius with grim satisfaction. "She broke into the attics at Chuff House and stole clothes. . . ."

"I did not steal," said Elizabeth hotly. "The clothes are mine."

"This is all very vulgar and distasteful," said the duchess. "Since this person appears to be your uncle, Miss Markham, pray leave as soon as possible and take him with you."

Elizabeth looked wildly from face to face. Would no one help her? Mrs. Burlington was biting her lip and looking at the ground, Mr. Burlington was studying the painted ceiling with fascinated interest, Mr. Seymour was red to the roots of his hair but would not meet Elizabeth's eye, and the Prescott brothers and Mr. Pargeter together with the young debutantes were all watching the scene with an air of suppressed excitement as if at a bearbaiting.

She bent her head in weary submission. It was of no use to appeal for help to a group of people who were, in the main, enjoying her humiliation.

"A minute," drawled Lord Charles. "Mr. Markham, when your niece arrived here, she was not only too thin, she had the marks of a recent beating on her back. How came she by those marks?"

"Elizabeth was beaten for a most heinous sin," said Julius, his pale eyes flashing. "She escaped from her room to which she had been confined for stealing food from the kitchens. She climbed over the roof like a hoyden. . . ."

"Your house is on the far side of Bramley," said Mr. Seymour suddenly, "on the London Road."

Julius nodded.

"By George, sir, do you realize what you have just said? A gently bred girl was so hungry she was forced to stoop to stealing food, then she was locked in her room, and then when she escaped — an escape which could well have cost her her life — she was found and beaten,

130

beaten so savagely that she still carries those marks. You are a disgrace to the cloth, sir. You are a monster."

He crossed the room to stand beside Elizabeth, his hands clenched into fists.

"That class of persons is always beating something or another," said the duchess. "Too tiresome. Please end this painful, vulgar scene immediately."

"No," cried Mr. Seymour. "I . . ."

"Enough, Bertram," said Lord Charles in a quiet, level voice. "I am well capable of protecting my own fiancée, although I share your outrage."

There was a universal gasp. Lady Jane and her mother looked daggers at Elizabeth. Elizabeth felt she had been struck deaf and dumb with shock. Patience and Prudence looked as if they had just swallowed several very large and bitter lemons. Mrs. Markham was puffing and blowing, the flounces on the bosom of her taffeta gown rising and falling.

Julius stood very still. He looked more shocked than anyone else in the room.

Bertram Seymour took a few steps away from Elizabeth. He felt silly. He had seen her clasped in Charles's arms when the storm had started to blow up, but when it looked as if she had no champions, he had quickly assumed Elizabeth and Charles had been startled into momentary indiscretion by the shock of the storm, and he had been on the point of offering to marry Elizabeth himself.

Lord Charles, who was well aware that his friend had been on the point of making a rash proposal, looked at him with a certain rueful expression of pity in his green eyes and said, "I did not mean to make the announcement so soon, Mr. Markham. I had meant to ask your permission. But now that I *have* met you, I can only advise you to take your leave from here as quickly as possible before I whip you myself."

"Elizabeth Markham is in my care, and you may not marry her without my permission," said Julius triumphantly. Patience and Prudence bridled and tossed their heads as if to say, "Now what do you think of *that?*"

"Oh, I really wouldn't do anything to stand in my way," said Lord Charles equably. "At the very least, I would hound you out of Bramley. I would certainly have you up in court charged with cruelty."

Julius tried to stare him down, but Lord Charles's gaze was green and implaccable. Julius thought of that pesky lawyer due to arrive back from the north. All he, Julius, could do was retreat and hope and pray that this marriage never would take place.

He drew himself up. "I have no wish to see this painful affair develop into a brawl," he said. His pale eyes rested malevolently on Elizabeth. "But mark my words, my lord, there will come the time when you will understand how badly she needs discipline. Come, my dears."

The guests fell back as he marched from the room with his wife panting after him and with Patience and Prudence trying to look as haughty as possible and failing miserably.

After they had left, there was a long silence. Then Lord Charles walked forward and said to Elizabeth, "Come, my dear, we have things to discuss."

"Charles!" cried the duchess. "We appreciate you have made a noble gesture, but you cannot possibly be contemplating allying the great name of . . ."

"Enough, Mama, I will speak to you later. Come, Elizabeth."

With heart beating hard, Elizabeth followed him from the room.

He led her into the library and closed the door behind them.

"Won't you sit down?" he asked, waving a hand toward a high-backed chair.

Elizabeth shook her head. "I am sure what we have to say to each other will not take very long, my lord. It was good and kind of you to pretend we are engaged. But I have no alternative but to return to my uncle's house."

"I was not pretending," he said. "The proposal was rather forced on me, I admit, but I think we should suit very well."

"Even if I could accept your proposal," said Elizabeth, trying to stop her voice from shaking, "I could not possibly stay here a moment longer. Your mother will be furious, not to mention Lady Jane."

"I am my own master, and what they say or do will not alter my decision one whit. But you are right. Have you no other relative who would take you in until the wedding?"

"No. None that I know of. I have, of course, various relatives throughout England, but I never really troubled to find out who they were. Mrs. Burlington told me Mr. Pargeter is related to me, but I had never even heard of him before. Uncle Julius was the only one I knew of, and he was approached by the lawyers immediately after my parents' death. But this is nonsense. I cannot marry you."

He took her hands and looked down intently into her face. "Surely you would rather marry me than return to your uncle?"

"Yes," said Elizabeth. "But I would not have you marry me out of kindness and compassion."

"It would not be quite that, my love, or have you forgotten last night so quickly?"

Elizabeth blushed and hung her head.

"You see? It will be quite easy to be married to me, so reconcile yourself to the idea. All you have to do is think of Uncle Julius. Now, no more protests. We must think of a plan. Mrs. Burlington travels direct to London this day in order to reside at her townhouse. Wait here, and I will go and ask her if she will take care of you in London until we are wed."

"But . . ."

He put a long finger against her lips.

"Not a word," he said. "I will take care of your future."

Elizabeth sank down into a chair after he had left. She could not stop her hands from trembling. It was almost impossible to believe that her worries and fears were over, that the stern threat of Uncle Julius had been dismissed.

After some moments, Lord Charles returned with a much-flustered Mrs. Burlington in tow.

"Of course we will be glad to chaperone you at the Season, Miss Markham," said Mrs. Burlington. "I thought at first, mind, that it was wicked of you to tell such lies, but Lord Charles pointed out that you were desperate and could not really do much else. Unfortunately, our townhouse is being redecorated. 'Tis most addlepated of me not to have had the house redecorated *before* the Season, but there you are. We have rooms at the Imperial Hotel so it is really no matter. I took the liberty of telling the servants to pack your bags because the duchess, your dear mama, Lord Charles, is in *such* a taking, and the other young ladies, well . . . 'tis best not repeated what *they* are saying!"

Mrs. Burlington prattled on about the arrangements for the journey, unfortunately letting slip that she and Mr. Burlington felt so beholden to Lord Charles for his expertise in ridding them of their unwanted servants that they felt compelled to oblige *him* by taking Elizabeth under their wing.

But Elizabeth was still so terrified at the idea of staying a moment longer with a furious duchess and her equally furious daughter that she could not summon up the courage to refuse Mrs. Burlington's offer.

Then it was Lord Charles's turn to explain that he would be traveling to London himself in two weeks' time and would then see that the notice of the engagement was inserted in all the papers.

And so Elizabeth was swept forward on a tide of arrangements. Fortunately for her peace of mind, Lady Jane was too furious with her to seek her out in her room and the few guests she met as she followed her trunks down the stairs pointedly turned their backs on her, all feeling that she had coerced Lord Charles, the biggest prize on the Marriage Mart, into marriage.

As the Burlingtons' carriage finally rolled south, bearing a dazed but relieved Elizabeth Markham on the long road to London, Julius Markham sat in his study, biting his nails and wondering what to do. It seemed unfair that Elizabeth Markham should inherit so much money when she would be marrying a lot of money. All he could finally think to do was to tell the lawyer of Elizabeth's forthcoming marriage and then plan and scheme ways to stop it before she learned of her inheritance.

First he must get his own servants to find out

from the duke's servants when they came shopping in the town just how the news of Lord Charles's engagement had been received by the family after he had left. The duke and duchess were well known for their obsession with the purity of their family name. Something must be done to stop that wedding. Perhaps a hint of madness? Something like that.

Two days after Elizabeth's departure, he received a visit from no less a personage than the duchess of Dunster herself. Dressed from head to foot in black as though in mourning and heavily veiled as if to protect her aristocratic face from such low surroundings, the duchess was ushered into Julius's dark and gloomy drawing room.

With an imperious wave of her hand, the duchess dismissed Mrs. Markham and her daughters, signifying she wished to be alone with Julius.

"This is a sad business, Mr. Markham," said her grace, fortifying herself with a far-from-delicate sniff at a silver-topped vinaigrette.

"Believe me, Your Grace, I feel the same."

"You amaze me," said the duchess. She put down the vinaigrette and fumbled in her bosom until she found her quizzing glass. She raised it to one eye and studied Julius's face, then dropped the glass quickly as if she had spied a beetle walking up his nose.

"Yes," smiled Julius, although he would dearly have loved to slap the duchess across her long nose and send her packing. "I fear you do not understand the circumstances. Were it not for Elizabeth's dangerous disposition, I would naturally be delighted that she had achieved such an exalted match."

"Dan—ger—ous," drawled the duchess. "*Dan*—ger—ous?"

"It is a delicate matter."

"Do not be so mealy-mouthed, Mr. Markham. You are not the type of person I would attribute any delicacy *to*. It naturally follows that any *person* so thoughtless of his place in life as to become a dissenting minister must naturally have no delicacy whatsoever. Now, *I*, I have a great deal of delicacy." She resorted to the vinaigrette once more while Julius regarded her balefully.

"Where is Elizabeth?" he demanded harshly.

"Alas, gone to London with that pushing, fat creature, Mrs. Burlington, to reside with her until the wedding."

"Odso! Our Elizabeth is very fortunate."

"Too fortunate. It was all Charles's doing. He must go and tell that Burlington *thing* to look after Elizabeth. He will follow her quite soon and then the damage will be irreparable."

Julius put his head down and covered his face with one long, bony hand. "Alas, poor Lord Charles."

The duchess began to feel alarmed. She had expected that Julius, after his initial show of wrath at the announcement of his niece's engagement, would have changed and now would be delighted at such a match. She felt piqued that such an unfashionable creature should appear to share her own exalted distress.

"Why do you keep mumbling and pitying my son?" she demanded. "And let us return to the matter of Miss Markham's soi-disant *dangerous* disposition."

"Your Grace," said Julius, raising his head, "you know that I may have appeared harsh in my treatment of Elizabeth."

"You do seem to have given the girl a sore beating."

"But that, Your Grace, if I may remind you, is an accepted treatment of one who is . . . *mad*."

"Mad? Mad! Oh, my poor Charles."

"Worse than that. Elizabeth has quite long periods when she appears sane. But she has the very cunning of the madwoman. He will not find out about her insane fits until she has him secure."

"I will tell him what you said."

"And what will that do? Your Grace, he will merely laugh in our faces and call me a vindictive man."

"Then what's to do?"

Julius thought rapidly. "I have — knowing Elizabeth so well — ways of promoting her madness, bringing it to the surface, so to speak. But that would mean leaving my flock and traveling to London."

"Then do so! I command you!"

"Forgive me, Your Grace. I am not yours to command."

The duchess stared about the dark, old furnishings of the room, nervously beating out a tattoo with the bloodless fingers of her left hand so that the great ruby on the ring she wore on her middle finger sent flashes of red light dancing over Julius's face.

"You do not have much money," she said. "That I can see."

Julius had, in fact, a great deal of money, but he liked to keep as much of it as possible safely in the bank.

"I will fund you . . . generously."

Julius studied his chalky nails. "It would grieve me to have to leave behind my wife and two daughters."

"Then take them by all means," cried the duchess. "We ourselves will be removing to town soon, and so I shall be on hand to witness your progress. Elizabeth is staying at the Imperial Hotel with the Burlingtons. I think it would be too obvious if you stayed there as well. You cannot stay with us, since people of our rank do not rub shoulders with people of yours. Find some modest lodgings, I pray."

"Your Grace," said Julius evenly. "I cannot possibly manage to meet Elizabeth at any social event of the Season if I am in modest lodgings. It is essential that my daughters should be invited to the best households. My name is as good as yours. . . ."

"Your calling puts you beyond the pale."

"As I said, as good as yours. We may forget about my calling in London. To put it bluntly, for this plan to work, you will not only need to fund me but make sure that I and my wife and daughters are socially acceptable during the Season."

The duchess gave a shudder and closed her eyes.

Julius sat there, patiently waiting, hating her.

"Very well," she said at last. "But only until the end is achieved. You are sure she is mad?"

"Oh, yes," said Julius gently. "Quite, quite mad, I assure you."

The Dunsters' stately butler at that moment was approaching Lady Jane with two sheets of parchment in his hand. "My lady," he said, "these writings were found under the desk in Miss Markham's room. Do you desire us to send them to her?"

"Let me see," said Jane, holding out her hand.

She stared down at the writing, and then a slow, rather malicious smile curled her lips. "No," she said slowly, "I think Lord Charles would like to deliver these papers to his fiancée personally."

Lord Charles Lufford was sitting in his private study, looking out of the window at the park, his chin in his hand, thinking about Elizabeth.

He could not wait to see her again. He forgot that he had once believed her an egotistical flirt. He did not know whether he loved her or not. He only wanted to be with her as soon as possible so that he might once more experience that warmth and desire and enchantment he had felt when he had last held her in his arms.

He had endured several wearing scenes, first with his father, then with his mother, and then with Jane. Bertram had wished him well, but in an awkward, hangdog way that had been most embarrassing. The rest of the guests had gone out of their way to show their displeasure at what they all seemed to consider a highly unsuitable alliance. Only Lady Herne had laughed lightly, patted his cheek, and wished him well.

When he turned and saw his sister standing in the doorway, he sighed, anticipating another scene.

"Since you will shortly be seeing Elizabeth in London," said Jane, "perhaps you might care to take these papers to her. They were found under the desk in her room."

"Very well." Lord Charles took the papers, and to Jane's dismay, he tucked them in the back of his dressing case without looking at them.

"I think you should read them, Charles. They concern you."

"I am not in the way of reading anyone else's private papers."

"Then you are a very great fool," raged Jane. "You have only to read what she has written to realize how you have been tricked and gulled."

She turned on her heel and slammed out of the room.

Lord Charles stood for a long time staring at his dressing case. Then with an exclamation of disgust, he picked up the papers.

In increasing fury and amazement, he read Elizabeth's notes on the male members of the house party. His own name seemed to leap out at him from the page. "Arrogant and spoilt by too much attention," he read, "and if he is as insufferably proud as his mother and sister, then he would be impossible to live with. In short, a complete waste of time."

The papers fell from his fingers. All in that moment of rage, he forgot that he himself had often considered both his mother and sister insufferably proud. He forgot about Elizabeth's desperate need to escape from her uncle. He realized only that he had been well on the way to loving her as he had loved no woman before, and that she had shamelessly tricked him into marriage . . . not by the arrival of her uncle, but by cunningly staging scenes and settings in such a way as to make him forget himself.

Somehow he would get his revenge.

But marry Elizabeth Markham, he would not!

He would see her in hell first.

Some little distance away from Lord Charles, in a room in the east wing, Mr. Derry Pargeter was gloomily opening a letter from his father.

He read the contents in increasing dismay. "My son," his father had written, "I cannot possibly fund your Gambling Debts any longer. I must once again plead with you to observe Moderation in All Things. Had it not been for this Fatal Tendency, this predilection for the gambling tables, then you might this day have been possessed of a fortune. A Distant Relative of Our Family, an old Eccentric, Giles Endicotte by name, had at one time thought of leaving you his money and Estate, although he had not seen you since you were a boy. But somehow he learned of your debts, for he wrote to me on that Matter before his Death. Instead, he has left his fortune to Miss Elizabeth Markham, who, I believe, resides in the vicinity of the Dunster Estates. God forbid anything should befall the girl, but should she die, you would then Inherit, for the old man retained some fondness for you. The man who marries her shall however gain control of her estate. I strongly advise you to consider marriage, if not to Miss Markham — since you are not closely related it would be allowable — then to some Heiress.

"Mrs. Pargeter is not in Plump Currant since the wind has moved to the East. We pray for a Good Harvest this year although . . ."

Derry Pargeter threw down the letter after rapidly skimming the rest of it in the hope that his parents might have relented further down the page and promised to send money.

Elizabeth Markham.

Did she know of her inheritance?

She could not know of it, yet else why had she been prepared to return to her uncle — whom she obviously feared and loathed — just before Lord Charles proposed marriage in that oblique way.

Damn Lord Charles. *He* had so much money, he didn't *need* any more. Mr. Pargeter was a very handsome man — and knew it. To date he had had little interest in the ladies, since he loved himself too well. But he was well aware of his attractions. Elizabeth Markham was not married yet. He would visit that horrible minister and fish about to see if Elizabeth knew about old Endicotte's money. If she did not, he might manage to woo her away from Lord Charles. Mr. Pargeter had seen Elizabeth and Lord Charles locked in a passionate embrace in the garden but was not dismayed by the remembrance of it. Having no very strong feelings in that direction himself, he found it impossible to credit anyone else with strong feelings and assumed Elizabeth had been wantonly trying to snare Lord Charles because he was the most likely suitor.

Mr. Pargeter studied his own face in the glass until he was reassured he was as beautiful as ever. He was convinced he was irresistible to women. Luring Miss Markham away from Lord Charles should be an easy matter. And after he was married to her, he would not have to see her much. He decided to leave immediately for London. Better to get there ahead of Lord Charles.

Then, of course, she might die. She was very fragile in appearance, and London was simply reeking with all sorts of humors, agues, and infections.

He imagined a typhoid epidemic sweeping through the West End of London so vividly that he began to whistle jauntily as he rang the bell and supervised the packing of his bags.

Lady Jane Lufford bit her fingernails in a most unladylike manner. Had stupid Charles read what Elizabeth had written? He could *not* marry such a treacherous snake as Elizabeth had turned out to be. Not only were there her common relatives — that was bad enough — but there was her nasty, cunning scheming. "She even pretended to be my friend," thought Jane.

It had been mildly amusing to see Elizabeth kissing Charles at the ball in that shameless way. She had thought Elizabeth had meant to make Mr. Seymour jealous.

Charles must be brought to realize the enormity of what he had done. But there was something so *vulgar* about Charles. When she had been a very little girl, she had hero-worshiped him. But he had gone away to the wars and had come back cold and harsh and seemingly determined to treat every man as his equal. If he married Elizabeth, it would be the same as becoming a Radical.

Jane decided to persuade her mother to leave for London as soon as possible. Getting rid of Elizabeth Markham would add a certain spice to life.

The ball had been so dull after the excitement of the storm had died down. Armies of servants had simply moved everything indoors to the large ballroom in the east wing. A footman had broken his leg when the marquee had blown away — one of the huge tent pegs had crashed into him — but no one who mattered had been at all hurt. No dramas.

Later that day, Julius Markham received another visitor. In great alarm and surprise, he heard Mr. Derwent Pargeter's claim that he was a relative. In even greater alarm, he heard Mr. Pargeter say that he knew the terms of old Endicotte's will. He would have been shocked to the core had Mr. Pargeter chosen to reveal the fact that he, Derwent Pargeter, would inherit should Elizabeth die.

But as Mr. Pargeter lied away about his love for Elizabeth and his plans to stop the marriage to Lord Charles, Julius began to see a gleam of hope.

147

He would assist this Mr. Pargeter in his plans. Mr. Pargeter was not nearly so formidable as Lord Charles. If Elizabeth should fall in love with Mr. Pargeter and break off the engagement, then Julius could easily step in and prove her mad before any other engagement took place. It would be very difficult to persuade a man like Lord Charles of Elizabeth's madness. Mr. Pargeter was another matter.

Julius decided to leave for London as soon as possible. He listened with half an ear to Mr. Pargeter's protestations of love while he planned to escape south before the arrival of the lawyer.

Let that lawyer find out where he was, where Elizabeth was. It would delay matters very nicely. If Julius *had* waited for the return of Mr. Thomson, then he might have found out about Mr. Pargeter's being the heir. But, as it was, he was only anxious to get away.

At last he promised Mr. Pargeter every help and sent that young man on his way.

His thoughts turned to Mrs. Battersby. She was turning out a most vindictive and tiresome woman. Perhaps it would be better to pay her that reward and bring her to London. If Elizabeth cried out that she had seen some cottager from Bramley who could be cleverly made to seem as if she did not exist, that would be first proof of her madness. There were so many plans to make. The main thing was to get to London and set them in motion.

Chapter Seven

Elizabeth had had much time to think about Lord Charles on the long journey south. Mrs. Burlington was plagued with travel sickness and for most of the journey lay back moaning gently with her eyes closed. Mr. Burlington was a marvelous sleeper. Elizabeth was constantly amazed at the way that gentleman could sleep for hours in a lurching, jolting carriage.

Every time Elizabeth thought of Lord Charles, she experienced a strange mixture of pain and sweetness somewhere in the pit of her stomach. She was sure he did not love her, but oh, she was so very sure she could make him do so! She never stopped to wonder whether *she* loved *him*. The earlier part of the journey flew past for Elizabeth, dazed as she was with relief. She could not quite think of Lord Charles as a person, as an individual, as a man. Rather she thought of him as a title, as a fortune, and as a rescuer.

As the carriage finally approached the outskirts of London, Elizabeth trembled with excitement.

London! The magic city full of glittering shops and balls and concerts.

But her excitement faded as they started to thread their way through the suburbs. Had these broken-down hovels always been there? Had the ragged children always played in black puddles in the mean streets?

Elizabeth felt she had seen enough of ugly streets and poverty. She did not want to *know* they were still there, although the scene before her was London and not Bramley.

Her excitement had dimmed, and she wished for the first time that she did not have to stay at the Imperial Hotel.

She would much rather Mr. and Mrs. Burlington had had their townhouse ready. She had never stayed at a hotel before and did not know what to expect.

Her spirits began to rise as the carriage finally rumbled over the well-paved streets of the prosperous West End. Opposite Green Park, the carriage turned into Clarges Street and stopped in front of the Imperial Hotel.

The Imperial was typical of a new breed of London hotel. A groom of the chambers and a lady's maid had invested their united earnings in a roomy mansion too much out of repair to serve as a private residence.

Then, by dint of showy calico, stained mahogany, and half the brass of a whole Birmingham foundry, they entitled themselves to demand, as rent for every suite of apartments, as much as the whole house would have cost if hired for the Season. Prodigious four-poster beds groaning with draperies and fringes were erected in the bedrooms with as much labor and ingenuity as were employed to run up a three-storey house in the suburbs. The rest of the bedroom furniture was made up of rickety wardrobes and washing stands purchased at cheap and nasty furniture brokers in the Blackfriars Road.

It was hazardous to open a drawer because three-quarters of an hour must be wasted in shoving, sliding, and swerving the ill-fitting drawer back into its original position. Frequenters of such London hotels learned the folly of trying to pull down a blind. They could hardly ever get it up again and the blind thus displaced or the drawer left sticking out at an angle was sure to be recalled to its guest's memory by a bill like the following:

	s	d
To man one day repairing Blind	17	6
Cords, &c., for do.	6	10
Easing drawer, strained	10	6

To touch the handle of a china or marble vase was equally hazardous. Pooloo's cement did not last forever. So if the guest found himself looking at the vase on the mantel while holding the handle in his hand, be sure he would be billed for the original cost of "handsome vase of Nankin Dragon China, finely enamelled." In this way a vase purchased damaged at a sale ten years before would have been paid for by twenty different victims, all inhabitants of the same unlucky suite.

The next object of the hotelkeeper was to purchase vast services of ironstone, which, in an emergency, when the families under his roof were sufficiently frantic or unfortunate to dine at home, he filled with beds of parsley, in the center of which, by dint of much examination with a powerful glass, could be discovered a thin slice of cod or salmon or a couple of fried whitings, a few chips of cutlets, a starveling cat roasted rabbitwise, or a brace of sparrows deluged in parsley and butter designated in the bill of fare as pigeons or chickens. The second course would probably be a bread pudding made from the crumbs that fall from a rich man's table or a tart apparently composed of buff leather or mouldy fruit. But all dishes were served under an embossed cover and in a lordly manner.

Not yet aware of the perils of dusty rooms and third-rate furniture that awaited them in their apartments upstairs, the Burlingtons and Elizabeth found their arrival at the Imperial delightful.

The hall was thronged with liveries of every dye, and milliners' baskets and jewelers' cases encumbered the lobby. A whole retinue of bowing and scraping servants assisted them inside. Tea was pressed on them to take downstairs while their apartments were made "comfortable."

There were a number of children staying at

the hotel, and so the street outside was crowded with every variety of itinerant showman — conjurers on stilts, tumblers, Punch or the fantoccini, bands, and dancing dogs.

To Elizabeth, the jolly bustle and noise made the grimness of Bramley whirl away out of her memory. She was an engaged lady. She was to "do" the Season. And her handsome and elegant lord of a fiancé would soon be traveling to join her.

It was only when they retired upstairs to their apartments that some of the disadvantages of hotel living began to make themselves felt. The first thing that was noticeable was the thinness of the partitions between the rooms. Elizabeth could hear Mr. Burlington complaining that the towels still smelled of their previous owner's use and had not been washed at all but simply screwed into a dry linen press.

Mrs. Burlington had brought only her lady's maid and Mr. Burlington his valet, so the luggage had to be unpacked by the hotel servants.

The two maids who unpacked and put away Elizabeth's belongings were very obsequious, almost embarrassingly so, but managed to convey to her nevertheless that they were surprised by her small wardrobe. Elizabeth had carefully left behind the clothes lent to her by Lady Jane, not wishing to draw any more accusations of stealing upon her head.

Next door Mr. Burlington was being mollified by the speed with which the staff were responding to his complaint about the towels, not knowing that the fat manager, seated in his office, was already adding the price of a whole new set of towels to his bill.

All was silent for a while, and then there was a scream from Mrs. Burlington and a loud crash. She had been preparing to send out various notes to announce her arrival in town and had sat down on the flimsy chair at the writing desk, only to have the chair collapse under her weight.

On the other side of the wall, the one away from the Burlingtons, Elizabeth heard a couple enter *their* rooms. The husband immediately began to berate his wife over her extravagance, and the wife burst into noisy tears.

Elizabeth would have liked a bath but had not the courage to ask the servants to carry one up the stairs.

She contented herself with a wash down while standing in a basin, only realizing when she was naked and sopping wet that she had failed to have her own towels changed. The previous user of the towels had been much addicted to a perfume called Miss in Her Teens but had fortunately not been very dirty. As she was rubbing herself down with the small towel, the door burst open and Mrs. Burlington sailed in. That lady's face turned a dull red as Elizabeth tried to disguise her nakedness with the towel. Mrs. Burlington turned her back.

"I shall turn round when you are decent," she said in a voice choked with embarrassment.

Elizabeth dragged on her clothes and told Mrs. Burlington that she might safely turn around.

"What on earth can you be thinking of!" exclaimed Mrs. Burlington.

"I know the towels are not very clean," said Elizabeth, "but I felt so gritty after the long journey."

"But there is no need to wash *all over*," said Mrs. Burlington. "Surely your poor mama warned you against the danger of rheumatics. It is such an unnatural thing to do. Every month or so is all very well, but you had a bath *last night* when we stayed at that posting house."

"My mother believed that cleanliness prevented infection."

"Pooh, pay no heed to such antiquated notions. And to be naked! *I* am never naked. I have a special gown I wear for bathing."

"Quite right, too," remarked the gentleman next door, leaving off berating his wife to join in the conversation.

"Oh, dear," wailed Mrs. Burlington. "I do wish our house was ready. Never mind. Lord Charles will know just what to do when he arrives. He always does."

"Where is my cravat," howled Mr. Burlington from the other side.

"He doesn't need to shout," said Mrs. Burlington. "He doesn't realize one has only to

155

speak in a whisper to be heard in the other room."

"Isn't that just what I said," complained the lady in the next room. "You should not shout so. Everyone can hear you."

"Who wants to hear *you?*" said her husband rudely. "You don't, do you?" he called to Mrs. Burlington and Elizabeth.

"Pay no attention," said Mrs. Burlington. "We had planned to spend a quiet evening here, but I do not think we are going to get much rest. I shall be so glad when dear Lord Charles arrives!"

Mrs. Burlington was to wish for Lord Charles's arrival many times in the following days.

Mr. Burlington remained somewhat of an enigma to Elizabeth. It did seem odd that as well as his wife, Mr. Burlington should wait patiently like a child for the arrival of Lord Charles to set things right instead of dealing with them himself.

Elizabeth had been embarrassed to find that Lord Charles had told Mrs. Burlington to arrange a new wardrobe of clothes for her. In vain had she protested. Mrs. Burlington had pointed out calmly that it was always better to do what Lord Charles said and enjoyed the shopping expeditions so immensely that Elizabeth finally had not the heart to refuse. The Burlingtons and Elizabeth were invited to various functions, but Mrs. Burlington had refused them all, saying there would be time enough to go to everything when Elizabeth's new clothes were ready. It also transpired that Mr. Burlington was writing a book on the Norman invasion of England and so he was buried in various libraries for most of the day.

The trouble was that they dined most evenings at the hotel while the manager rubbed his hands and marked down brill in the ledger as turbot and kept the heads of woodcocks and pheasants as sacred as that of the Baptist in order to consecrate dishes of hashed mutton so that they might appear as *salmis de bécasse* or *de faisan.*

But life in the hotel had its advantages. It offered Mrs. Burlington relief from the cares of housekeeping. The waiters and servants were always courteous and prompt to answer bells. Every ring ensured expenditure, varying from twelve pence to a guinea. Coals, a sandwich, even a candle to seal a letter were all added to the bill, and as the Burlingtons did not know this yet, they were tolerably comfortable. It seemed, however, that they still mourned the absence of Lord Charles because they believed that he would, in some mysterious way, render the dinner dishes more palatable and thicken the walls between the rooms.

Elizabeth's first caller was Mr. Pargeter. As she was rather lonely, having only Mrs. Burlington for company, she welcomed this gentleman who was so much nearer her own age. He was even more handsome than she remembered, and he had lost that acidulous manner. Mrs. Burlington was rather startled at Mr. Pargeter's request to take Elizabeth driving in the park, but when it appeared that Mr. Pargeter was fully aware of Elizabeth's engagement to Lord Charles and when he professed that he was simply entertaining a relative, Mrs. Burlington gave way and allowed Elizabeth to go.

Mr. Pargeter had decided to establish a friendship with Elizabeth first, before trying to turn it into something warmer. He had to stay close to her so as to discover the best way to drive a wedge between her and Lord Charles. Elizabeth, not knowing of her inheritance, would only be too glad to marry the next man who asked her after her engagement was broken.

He chatted away about this and that as they drove around Hyde Park. Elizabeth could not help noticing the glances of envy she was receiving from various young ladies in the other carriages. She was flattered at the way Mr. Pargeter appeared not to notice the interest he was causing and the way in which he gave her his whole attention.

Mrs. Burlington questioned Elizabeth closely on her return, and finding out that Mr. Pargeter was obviously as innocent as he seemed, she gave Elizabeth permission to drive out again with him on the following day.

Their friendship grew. Elizabeth ignored a little voice inside her head that told her that there was something a little strange about Mr. Pargeter's constant attention.

One day, while they were again driving through the park, Elizabeth saw an open carriage bowling toward her at a smart pace. In it sat her uncle Julius with Mrs. Markham and Prudence and Patience. She turned very white and clutched at Mr. Pargeter's sleeve. "Look!" she whispered.

He looked this way and that, wondering what had upset her, but he did not notice the Markham carriage as it bowled past. The Markhams stared straight ahead and did not seem to see Elizabeth.

"It was my uncle Julius," said Elizabeth, "with the family. They just passed us."

"You must be imagining things," said Mr. Pargeter, twisting his neck around. "I didn't see them."

"But you wouldn't remember them," said Elizabeth, white to the lips. "They did not see me. They must be in London looking for me. I know it!"

"Nonsense. There is no reason for them to be here. You imagined it," said Mr. Pargeter. "I say, you're not going to faint, are you? He can't do anything anyway with me to protect you."

Elizabeth gave him a grateful smile but wondered why Mr. Pargeter did not say anything about Lord Charles. He appeared to have forgotten his very existence.

Mr. Pargeter set himself to amuse Elizabeth and succeeded so well that she was almost convinced, by the time they returned to the hotel, that she had indeed imagined seeing the Markham family.

She was laughing gaily at something Mr. Pargeter was saying as she walked into the hall when all at once she saw the tall figure of Lord Charles Lufford standing glaring at her. He looked so tall and angry that her eyes flew instinctively to Derry Pargeter for help, a look that was not lost on Lord Charles.

His green eyes took in the splendor of her outfit, an outfit that *he* had paid for. She was wearing a high-waisted, ankle length dress of rose-colored muslin. The sleeves were short and puffed, and she wore long suede gloves of a darker rose. On her head was a frivolous capote hat ornamented with rose ribbons.

Mr. Pargeter was dressed in the Brummell fashion, in a buff-colored coat, the sleeves gathered and padded at the top to give the "kick-up" effect. The top buttons of his waistcoat were left undone to reveal a delicate cambric shirt frill, and the collar of his starched shirt rose high enough around his cheeks to earn it the nickname of "the patricide." Together, he and Elizabeth looked like a fashion plate from *La Belle Assemblée* — and very well matched.

Behind Lord Charles stood the Burlingtons. Mrs. Burlington's fat face was creased into lines of dismay, and Mr. Burlington was moodily studying the toes of his own boots.

"You will forgive us, Mr. Pargeter," said Lord Charles icily. "I wish to have a word in private with *my fiancée.*"

Mrs. Burlington looked at Lord Charles in distressed surprise. For had not Lord Charles just been fuming and fretting and saying the engagement was at an end because Elizabeth had tricked him into it? And had she not herself been forced to confess to some doubts about Elizabeth, and hadn't she even told Lord Charles about how Elizabeth had said her uncle was a bishop when, in fact, he was nothing more than a dissenting minister? Now she felt as if she had been disloyal to Elizabeth.

But Mr. Pargeter was already making his farewells, and Lord Charles barely let Elizabeth wait to hear them before marching her upstairs to the Burlingtons' private sitting room.

Elizabeth began to tremble as soon as Lord Charles closed the door behind them. She did not feel like a young lady alone with her fiancé after an absence but more like a bullied child facing a stern parent.

"Now Elizabeth," said Lord Charles awfully, "what have you to say to this?"

He held out the two sheets of parchment on which Elizabeth had set down her impressions of the gentlemen of the house party.

"I'm sorry," said Elizabeth, hanging her head. She had known for some time that she had left the papers behind but assumed the servants would throw them away. "You must understand, my lord, I was terrified of having to return to Uncle Julius. I felt I must find someone to marry me, and yes, I did think you too spoiled by attention, and you must admit your mother and sister are very, very proud, and . . ."

"And so you tricked me into offering to marry you. God knows I only did it to save Bertram from making a fool of himself. He should be grateful to me, considering *he* was your target and not I. I have informed the Burlingtons that our engagement is at an end."

"How could I trick you?" demanded Elizabeth, rage giving her courage. "I did not know that Uncle Julius would call. As a matter of fact, I had already decided the whole plan was silly and would not work. I did not know what to do. Oh, I only wish you had seen me first instead of distressing poor Mrs. Burlington."

"If you had had more concern for 'poor' Mrs. Burlington, then you might not have told her so many lies. Bishop, indeed!"

"I was afraid that if it were discovered my uncle was a Nonconformist minister, then I should most definitely have been sent packing.

"Oh, you do not know what it was like. When Mrs. Burlington picked me up at the gate, I did not think of marriage. All I wanted was food. Lots and lots of food. I was so very hungry."

He studied her narrowly, remembering that

first breakfast, recalling how she had eaten like someone who had not had a decent meal in weeks.

"There was no need to propose to me in order to save Mr. Seymour," said Elizabeth. "I am sure I would not have married him when it came to the bit."

"But in the meantime you would have broken his heart."

"I am not capable of breaking anyone's heart," said Elizabeth.

He looked into her wide eyes and saw that she thought she spoke the truth.

"I am very sorry that I have cost you so much money for . . . for the clothes," went on Elizabeth, miserably. "I will return them. . . ."

"Do not be silly. I have no need for fripperies."

"But when you *do* marry . . ."

"You are mad. I shall of course say to my wife, 'Here, take these gowns and ribbons which I bought for my last fiancée.' "

"What am I to do?" said Elizabeth wretchedly. "I am terrified of Uncle Julius. Mr. Pargeter is some kind of distant relation. Perhaps his parents . . ."

"No. I do not wish you to go about with Derry Pargeter either."

"But if our engagement is at an end."

"What an infuriating woman you are. Did I say it was?"

"I believe you told the Burlingtons so."

163

"Of course I told the Burlingtons. Any man would be in a rage over that mischievous nonsense you wrote down. Any man in his senses, that is . . . Oh, Elizabeth."

He took a step toward her when a voice from the next room said sweetly, "Oh no, you don't, young man. I know what is going on in there, and if you are only engaged, I won't allow it."

"Who the devil are you?" demanded Lord Charles wrathfully.

"I am Lady Eccles."

"Old trout," muttered Lord Charles. "Well, Lady Eccles," he said, raising his voice, "may I suggest that you pretend the walls are thicker and endeavor to mind your own business."

"The morality of others *is* my business."

"Oh, take your ear away from the wall, you old harridan," said Lord Charles, and as an outraged squawk came from next door, he said gently to Elizabeth, "I feel I have been too hasty. Let us go back to the poor Burlingtons and let the engagement stand. We shall not announce it officially yet, for I feel we should spend some time together first. We are barely acquainted."

"Worse and worse," said Lady Eccles from the other side of the wall.

Lord Charles picked up a vase and threw it at the wall. Outside, the waiter took his ear away from the door and ran down the stairs to the manager's office, and the manager promptly entered "one vase, Ming period" on to Mr.

Burlington's account.

At first Mrs. Burlington was not very pleased at the news of the reconciliation. Such "ons and offs" made her head ache, she said. But when Lord Charles moved on to the subject of their accommodation and said he knew of a very pleasant townhouse that had just become available for letting and that he was sure he could secure it for them, Mrs. Burlington melted and called him the very best of men.

Lord Charles went off to attend to the matter, and Elizabeth was left feeling exhausted after all the seesawing emotions of the day.

Like the Burlingtons, she was, nonetheless, immensely relieved that Lord Charles had arrived to take charge. And she could not possibly have seen her uncle in the park.

They were transferred in a mere two days' time to a charming townhouse in Charles Street. Lord Charles had also reduced the hotel bill to half the price the manager had demanded. Since servants were not part of the lease, Mrs. Burlington was able to have her own staff. She announced they were now ready to attend some of the delights of the Season. She had accepted invitations to a ball given that very evening by Lady Maxwell. Wasn't Lord Charles wonderful? He never seemed to have any worries.

But at that very moment Lord Charles was very worried indeed. He had called at his father's townhouse in Grosvenor Square to find his mother entertaining Julius Markham and his family to tea. His mother was being extremely gracious, and even sister Jane was smiling pleasantly on the horrible Markham sisters.

He could barely contain his temper until they had left. But when he berated his mother on her choice of guests, she replied with a fond smile that *he* was too high in the instep and that she found Julius Markham a very good sort of man and had persuaded Lady Maxwell to give the minister and his family invitations to her ball — not that she had dared to mention his Nonconformist calling.

"This is the outside of enough, Mama," raged Lord Charles. "You are playing some deep game with that horrible man in order to find some way to terminate my engagement to Elizabeth."

"Not I," said the duchess with such mock surprise that Lord Charles ground his teeth.

"I am making the best of things. Since you are so set on this marriage, I am doing the correct thing by being pleasant to Elizabeth's family."

"I don't believe a word of it," said Lord Charles. "Elizabeth will be most upset when she learns that man is in London. I shall persuade her not to go to the ball this evening."

But, as it turned out, Elizabeth, after the initial shock of learning that her uncle was indeed in London, said she was determined to go to the Maxwells. "You must see," she said, "that I cannot hide from him forever."

And so Lord Charles let her have her way.

Elizabeth looked beautiful in a gown of delicate white silk embroidered with golden ears of wheat. She wore a simple coral necklace about her neck and white silk flowers decorated the burnished tresses of her golden hair.

When she saw Lord Charles in evening dress, she could not help wondering why she had ever thought Derry Pargeter handsome.

And as she looked at her fiancé, she also could not help feeling some sympathy with his family. In a way, she had trapped him. If only she had some money so that she could say to him, "I can look after myself. Now do you still wish to marry me?"

Lord Charles noticed the doubtful look in her eyes and wondered whether she was regretting the engagement. His next thought was "How dare she?" He still set a very high value on himself and could not get used to the fact that Elizabeth might feel she had to marry him because she had really no alternative.

Mrs. Burlington looked anxiously from one to the other, sensing the strained atmosphere, and hoped the wretched engagement was not going to be called off again.

She decided she did not really understand Elizabeth. At times she seemed such a comfortable sort of girl and at others strained and haunted.

The ball was very grand, and everyone who was anyone was there. Elizabeth had the doubtful pleasure of seeing Prudence and Patience sitting among the wallflowers, while she herself never lacked a partner. But the very presence of Uncle Julius made Elizabeth nervous. It was amazing enough that he was actually present at the Season. It was even more amazing that he should have managed to engineer invitations to this ball.

It was when Elizabeth at last found herself in Lord Charles's arms and moving to the strains of a waltz that she began to feel warm, protected, and secure.

She looked up at Lord Charles, trying to find words to thank him for saving her from Uncle Julius. His head turned slightly from her. He was looking across the room to where Lady Herne was smiling at him.

Elizabeth experienced a stab of jealousy and looked fixedly across his left shoulder.

That was when she saw Mrs. Battersby.

Mrs. Battersby was finely dressed and was wearing a velvet turban on her head.

Elizabeth stumbled over Lord Charles's feet.

"It's her," she said. "Mrs. Battersby."

"Who?"

"A woman, a very poor woman I used to visit when I was doing my parish rounds in Bramley."

"Don't look so shaken. Many countrywomen become servants in London."

"She was finely dressed. Look, there she . . ." Elizabeth's voice trailed away.

"She's gone," she said. "Please help me look for her. I must know what she is doing here. It was that woman, you know, the woman at the fair. I pretended I did not recognize her, for I knew she would tell my uncle. But that was Mrs. Battersby."

She broke away from him and almost ran to where Mrs. Battersby had been standing. But there was no sign of the woman from Bramley. Followed by Lord Charles, Elizabeth searched here and there, but the elusive Mrs. Battersby appeared to have disappeared into thin air.

"You must be imagining things," said Lord Charles, rather crossly. Elizabeth's next partner was heading toward them. She gave Lord Charles a bewildered look. "I *must* have seen her," she said. "I must. Only consider how I thought I imagined seeing Uncle Julius in the park, and yet, since he is *here*, it must have been him."

"Elizabeth, you are becoming incoherent. People are staring at you."

Elizabeth threw him a glance of mute reproach as she was led off into the next dance by her new partner.

Lord Charles went off to find some refreshment and came across Mr. Bertram Seymour.

"I say, Charles," said Mr. Seymour awkwardly. "There is some very odd gossip about Miss Markham circling the ball."

"Since her horrible uncle is present, not to mention his Friday-faced daughters, I have no doubt of it. What are they saying?"

"Well, there are whispers that she has mad fits."

"The devil!"

"People are whispering that she *sees* things and becomes violent."

Lord Charles felt a twinge of unease. Elizabeth had certainly behaved most oddly and had claimed to have seen some woman from Bramley.

He shook his head as though to clear it. "I assure you, Bertram, this hall seems full of people who do not want us to marry. There is her family and my family, and that's only a beginning. I saw the wretched Pargeter hovering about."

"Pargeter? Pargeter's only got time for his own reflection."

"Ah, but it would amaze you the way he dances attendance on Elizabeth."

"She has such charm," said Mr. Seymour awkwardly, "that even men who are not normally interested in the fair sex are forced to change their ways."

"Elizabeth was not for you," said Lord Charles gently. "She was flirting with us all so blatantly because she was terrified to return to that uncle of hers and thought marriage was the only solution."

"You must not feel *obliged* to marry," said Mr. Seymour. "It is not as if you are the only man who wants to marry her."

"You don't want to marry her, Bertram, believe me. You are very susceptible. You always were."

"Perhaps," said Bertram moodily.

Out in the ballroom, Elizabeth had become aware of a certain atmosphere emanating from the crowd around her. Eyes looked at her slyly, heads were bent, voices gossiped. Lady Jane watched her, her green eyes narrowed like a cat's. Prudence and Patience put their heads together and giggled.

Then there was a rustling and murmuring of excitement from the groups about the entrance. The great Mr. Brummell had arrived.

He was impeccably dressed as usual, and his fine hair was curled into artistic disarray. His turned-up nose, which had been that way ever since a horse kicked it, lent his face a mischievous look. Heads bobbed about him, and low voices relayed the latest on-dit about the strange Miss Markham. Then the crowd of admirers parted. The famous Beau raised his quizzing glass and studied Elizabeth with interest.

Julius Markham looked startled and dismayed as Mr. Brummell asked Elizabeth for the next dance. At the other side of the ballroom, Mrs. Burlington was anxiously asking

Lord Charles if he had heard all the malicious gossip about Elizabeth being mad.

"You must pay no heed, Mrs. Burlington," sighed Lord Charles. "Only see how balefully Mr. Markham is watching her. Of course he set such rumors about."

Lord Charles left that lady reassured, but he could not help wondering if Mrs. Burlington was a fit chaperone for Elizabeth. She was a kind, friendly woman, but she did seem to believe the last person who had spoken to her, and her loyalty to Elizabeth did not seem very strong. Lord Charles did not know that Mrs. Burlington and her husband had the perfect marriage because both of them were amiable and very lazy. They were quite prepared to be friendly and hospitable just so long as no particular effort was required.

Elizabeth was looking more relaxed, and yes, she was actually laughing at something the Beau was saying to her.

Lord Charles felt his heart give a lurch, and all at once he wished passionately that she would always look so carefree.

At the end of the dance he went to claim her. The Beau wandered off to join his admirers. He said a few words to them and waved his quizzing glass in the direction of Elizabeth. Whatever he said must have been flattering, for that odd gossiping hostility that Elizabeth had sensed died away. Once more she felt secure with her fiancé beside her.

"Supper is being served," said Lord Charles at the end of the dance. "Are you still as hungry as you were when I met you at that breakfast?"

"Almost," laughed Elizabeth.

"Then we must find you something to eat, and you can tell me all about that terrible household of your uncle's. You have never really had a chance to tell me how bad it was."

"Later," said Elizabeth with a shudder. "I don't even want to think about it now."

"It seems," said the duchess of Dunster behind her fan to Julius Markham, "that your plots and plans are a waste of time. Brummell has pronounced her charming, and he carries great weight. You, on the other hand, are of little consequence. You are, in fact, insignificant."

Julius flushed with rage at the insult. But he said in a very controlled voice, "My plans for this evening have only just begun."

The duchess sniffed contemptuously as he walked away.

Julius made his way to where Patience was sitting — Prudence had actually found a beau — and whispered to her, "Step aside. There is a little job you must do for me."

"You will start a new fashion, my sweeting," Lord Charles was saying to Elizabeth. "All these ladies who maintain the fiction of eating like birds will follow your example and eat as well as trenchermen."

"I still *do* get so very hungry," said Elizabeth. "And thirsty. Oh, do look. There is awful Patience waving and grimacing at me." Lord Charles looked around and followed her gaze. He put a hand over hers. "Don't look," he said. "Look at me instead. I think we should avoid functions where your relatives are going to be present."

Elizabeth's hand seemed to take fire from the feel of his own on top of hers. She felt such a strong suffocating wave of emotion that she was afraid to meet his eyes.

"Oh," she said, trying to laugh, "someone has put a jug of lemonade on the table. The very thing!"

"It is going to be a sad marriage if all you can think of is food and drink," he laughed, filling up her glass.

"Did you put the chloral in it?" asked Julius Markham.

"Yes, Papa," said Patience. "I handed it to the footman to take over and then attracted her attention."

"How much did you put in?"

"The whole bottle."

Julius scowled. "Let us hope it does not kill her."

Elizabeth had just drained one large glass of lemonade. She wrinkled her nose a little at the strange taste. Lord Charles poured her another glass, and she drank that, too.

Elizabeth slowly put down the glass. The

supper room had become very strange. Everyone looked so very far away, as if she were looking at them through the wrong end of a telescope.

She blinked to focus her eyes and found herself in the drawing room of Chuff House. Sitting across the table from her was Uncle Julius.

"No!" she screamed suddenly. "Oh, no!"

"What is it?" demanded Lord Charles. "Why are you looking at me like that?"

Elizabeth shrank away from him. She got to her feet, clutching hold of the table for support. "Help me," she pleaded wildly. "Please help me. Someone save me from this man. I've got to get away. *Must* get away!"

In her chloral-induced nightmare, Elizabeth felt herself being taken in a strong grasp. She was going to be locked in her room again. She struggled and fought like a demon. Glasses and dishes went flying from the table.

"Stop that!" said Lord Charles, shaking her roughly.

Elizabeth looked at him with haunted eyes and screamed and screamed.

Chapter Eight

Apart from the fact that there was no hatchment over the door, the Burlingtons' townhouse looked as if someone had died within. The blinds were drawn, and straw had been laid on the street outside to dull the rumble of passing traffic.

There was a death, however, in a kind of way, a social death, the death of Elizabeth Markham's reputation.

She had been carried to the carriage the evening before, screaming and struggling. Lord Charles had held her tightly while curious guests flocked outside the Maxwells' mansion to watch them drive away. Elizabeth had fallen unconscious a few moments after the carriage had rolled away.

A physician was routed from his bed to take a look at her. He had shaken his head and said that she was not unconscious but heavily asleep, as was usually the case with mad people after they had had a violent attack.

So once more Elizabeth was locked in her room. She did not awaken the following day until the sun was high in the sky. She felt weak and thirsty. No one came when she rang the bell. She tried the door and found it locked.

Elizabeth sat down on the edge of the bed,

her head in her hands. The nightmare was beginning again. She rushed to the window and looked out to reassure herself she was still at the Burlingtons and had not been transported in her delirium back to Chuff House.

Slowly and painfully she began to piece the evening of the ball together in her mind.

She remembered the nodding, gossiping faces and then the dance with the famous Beau Brummell. Mrs. Battersby! What on earth could Mrs. Battersby have been doing, grandly dressed, at Lady Maxwell's ball? It could not have been she. It simply *must* have been some woman bearing a remarkable resemblance to her. Lord Charles had taken her in to supper. Patience had been grimacing in that odd way. Elizabeth remembered feeling very thirsty. She had drunk two large glasses of lemonade, and that was when the nightmare had begun. She could not remember leaving the ball, getting home, going to bed.

Whatever she had done must have been terrible, because here she was, locked up. There was a click and the door opened.

Mrs. Burlington popped her head around the door. "My dear," she said, addressing the fireplace and not looking at Elizabeth. "Lord Charles is come with *two* physicians. He is in such a taking. He says the poor man we called in before was a quack. I shall send the maid to help you dress."

"No, thank you," said Elizabeth. "I will dress

myself. I am quite used to it, you know."

Hearing Elizabeth's calm, normal voice, Mrs. Burlington looked at her for the first time. "You are quite yourself again! What a terrible fright you did give me — ranting and raving. I said to Lord Charles it must be all that washing. I thought it had softened your brain. But he seems to take as many baths as you! I do not know what the world is coming to."

Mrs. Burlington bustled off, and Elizabeth dressed hurriedly and rang the bell when she had finished.

Lord Charles, she was told by the two physicians who entered, was below awaiting their verdict. One was old and one was quite young, and both were very deferential. They asked her politely to describe her symptoms and then asked her how she felt at that moment. While Elizabeth talked, the younger one sat at the writing desk and made copious notes. After about half an hour, they appeared satisfied and took their leave.

Elizabeth waited nervously. At last a footman scratched at the door and told her that Lord Charles wished to see her. He was waiting in the small saloon on the first floor. "It appears," he said, "that the learned gentlemen have both come to the conclusion that you were simply very drunk last night, and your subsequent symptoms this morning bear that out."

"I was not drunk," said Elizabeth. "I do not know what happened, except that everything became like a nightmare after I had drunk that lemonade."

"Meaning that there was something in the lemonade? Your uncle is a nasty man but hardly a Borgia, I think."

"But I did not drink very much," said Elizabeth. "I had two glasses of champagne before we left here. That was all."

She looked at him pleadingly. He seemed remote, his eyes guarded. Only now that it was not there did she realize he usually looked at her with a certain affectionate warmth in his green eyes.

"Please," she begged, "I was neither drunk nor mad. What will happen now?"

"I will try to repair the damage done to your reputation," he said, crossing to the window and standing with his back to her. "It would be awkward for the poor Burlingtons if you were to attend any social function with them at present."

"Perhaps . . . perhaps we could take a drive in the park," said Elizabeth. She wanted to escape this feeling of being confined to the house.

"Unfortunately that will not be convenient," said Lord Charles, still looking out of the window. "I have certain matters that need my attention."

"Oh," said Elizabeth in a dismal little voice. "I had forgot. You will naturally not wish to be seen with me either."

"That is not the case," he said with a certain

amount of asperity in his voice. "I would have thought that after your experiences, you would be happy to enjoy a quiet day at home."

"Home?" said Elizabeth bleakly. "Sometimes I wonder if I shall ever have a home again."

"My dear girl," said Lord Charles, swinging about, "you are shortly to be married to me, and . . ."

He broke off in consternation. He had been on the point of adding, "and you should consider yourself very lucky." Was he really as bad as his mother? He turned back to the window and looked down into the street.

"The devil," he said coldly. "Here is that fop, Pargeter, come to call."

"I am glad that at least one of my beaux has decided not to shun me," said Elizabeth.

"I was not aware you considered Pargeter a beau. Once a flirt, always a flirt."

"If *he* offers to take me driving, I shall go," said Elizabeth defiantly. She desperately wanted to hurt Lord Charles as much as he had just hurt her. Had not he more or less admitted he was so ashamed of her that he did not even want to be seen with her in the park?

"Then I bid you good day, madam, and wish you the joy of that counterjumper's company."

Lord Charles strode from the room, banging the door behind him. He swept past Mr. Pargeter, who was waiting in the hall, without even giving him a glance.

Outside in the street, he paused and wondered whether or not to go back. Why on earth had he not told her he was determined to find out more about her uncle? Why had he not let her know that that was the reason he had not time to take her driving? "Perhaps you are in love with her?" said a little voice inside his head. But he strode on before that uncomfortable voice could say any more. Elizabeth's strange behavior at the ball *had* to be explained before he entertained any softer emotion toward her. He had always prided himself on being a hardheaded practical man. Pargeter was nothing. Let her have her drive with Pargeter if that was the reason the young man was calling. He did not consider that weakling a rival. But he had a nasty lurching feeling inside as he pictured Pargeter and Elizabeth together. He was hungry. Of course, *that* was why he felt so odd and unhappy and worried. There was not a single problem that could not be solved with a beefsteak and a good bottle of claret. Mr. Markham could wait until the afternoon. Lord Charles headed toward Saint James's Street.

He would, however, have been very concerned if he could have seen the tender glance his fiancée was giving Mr. Derry Pargeter at that moment. For Mr. Pargeter had stoutly declared he was convinced there had been something nasty in the food or drink that had accounted for Elizabeth's hysterical behavior. He had added lightly that Mr. Markham was enough to give anyone of any sensibility the strong hysterics and he had asked her to accompany him on a drive.

"You see, Miss Markham," said Mr. Pargeter, "I really do think it best for you to be seen in public as soon as possible. That way, everyone will immediately see there is nothing wrong with you, and the whole scandal will soon be forgotten. Worst thing you could do is to hide indoors. Wonder Lord Charles didn't think of that."

Elizabeth gave him a warm smile but forbore from saying that she too wondered why Lord Charles had not suggested the same thing.

Mrs. Burlington's permission was asked, and that good lady gave it gladly. Elizabeth looked so much her normal self Lord Charles had warmly thanked both the Burlingtons for their loyalty to Elizabeth, and so Mrs. Burlington was only too anxious to see "everything comfortable again as she told herself. Lord Charles had been very upset about Elizabeth's last outing with Mr. Pargeter, but he had seen Mr. Pargeter waiting for Elizabeth because her maid had informed her of that fact, so it followed that Lord Charles must have given his blessing to the drive.

Mr. Pargeter was buoyed up by Elizabeth's warmth toward him. He did not consider for one moment that he was doing a very noble thing by being seen in public with this young lady who had disgraced herself so badly at the

Maxwells' ball. Mr. Pargeter wanted Elizabeth's inheritance, and when he wanted something, everything else paled to insignificance beside that want. He had once walked through a raging blizzard to get to a game of hazard at White's, barely noticing the cold or discomfort.

In fact, Mr. Pargeter would have been the bravest of England's soldiers had he ever enlisted, provided his colonel told him there was a good card game going on the other side of the enemy lines.

Oblivious to stares and raised quizzing glasses, he tooled his carriage among the fashionables in Hyde Park, rattling away, telling jokes and anecdotes to such good effect that it was marked by one and all that the mysterious Miss Markham was not only in high spirits and had all her wits about her but looked beautiful enough to stop the traffic. Before the physicians' visit, Lord Charles had been busy putting it about that his fiancée had had a *crise de nerfs* owing to her ill treatment at the hands of her uncle, and society was in its fickle way prepared to be kind.

After a little while he maneuverd his carriage away from the throng to a quieter and less-fashionable part of the park. Elizabeth was feeling elated. No one had cut her. It was like a miracle! She felt she owed it all to Mr. Pargeter, unaware that Mr. Pargeter was responsible only for a little bit of it. Lord Charles's careful groundwork had done most of it, combined with the fact that society was used to eccentrics and to members of the ton who behaved disgracefully when in their cups. In fact most gentlemen took a servant with them when they dined out, the servant's function being to stand behind the master's chair and scoop him tactfully out from under the table when he drank too much. Any servant incapable of covering up his master's drunkenness was fired on the spot, accused of drunkenness himself!

Mr. Pargeter noticed the warm and affectionate glances Elizabeth was casting at him and felt the time was right to press his suit. She had obviously had a tearing row with Lord Charles. Only see how Lord Charles had cut him, Derry Pargeter, dead, and no one would surely do that unless he were in the grip of some strong emotion. Probably Lord Charles had already terminated the engagement.

Mr. Pargeter slowed his team to a halt under the shade of a spreading oak and turned to Elizabeth. "Forgive me for being so personal, Miss Markham, but you will shortly see that I have a good reason for being so. I gather you have no money of your own."

"Not a penny," said Elizabeth, her brow clouding.

"And no prospects?"

"No, Mr. Pargeter, none."

"It was most opportune, then, when Lord Charles proposed marriage."

"Yes, it was."

"You had no other choice but to accept?"

"Well, that is perhaps the case, but . . ."

"It is as I thought," said Mr. Pargeter triumphantly. "Miss Markham . . . Elizabeth . . . *dearest* Elizabeth, I beg you to be mine. I love you with all my heart."

"Mr. Pargeter! You must not, I beg you. Remember I am engaged to Lord Charles."

"Who does not want you any more than you want him!"

"No," said Elizabeth slowly, as if realizing something for the first time. "I do want him. You see, I love him."

Her large blue eyes misted over. Of course, she thought, I do love him. I think I have loved him a very long time.

Mr. Pargeter stared at her in blind fury. He did not like rejection at the best of times. But this wretched female should have cast herself at his feet in gratitude. She was deceitful and mercenary. She naturally could not find Lord Charles more attractive than himself. Then it followed that she was determined to keep him to the engagement because she wanted not only his fortune but his title as well. Mr. Pargeter had never really liked women. But he felt at that moment that he had never hated any woman as much as he hated Elizabeth Markham.

Elizabeth was still dizzy with the realization that she loved Lord Charles. The fear that he would never love her would not come until later.

In a dream she heard Mr. Pargeter, very stiffly on his stiffs, say that they should return home.

When they arrived, Mr. Pargeter told her to get down from the carriage herself. Elizabeth realized she had not thanked him for his bravery in escorting her and turned on the pavement to do so, but Mr. Pargeter was already driving away at a smart pace.

Derry Pargeter arrived at his modest lodgings in Jermyn Street to find a dun awaiting him on the doorstep. The man was loud-voiced and importunate, and Mr. Pargeter was forced to pay him part of the money he owed him. He kicked some of the clutter of his sitting room aside and sank down into an easy chair in front of the fire.

He would need to go back home and rusticate. No more would he hear the magic clatter of dice or see those jolly playing cards spread out on the green baize. In two days' time there would be a new moon, and Mr. Pargeter knew his luck always ran high at the new moon.

What a pity Elizabeth could not drop dead. He weaved several rosy fantasies, envisaging Elizabeth dropping dead in the middle of Almack's. Once she was dead, then the lawyers would advance him the necessary sum.

But she had looked disgustingly healthy. Pity that uncle of hers hadn't beaten her to death. Mind you, if anything happened to her, people would blame the uncle. The more he thought of that idea while gambling fever raged in his veins, the more Mr. Pargeter began to think it might be a very good thing to assist Elizabeth Markham into the next world.

Lord Charles had spent an exhausting afternoon closely questioning his mother about her odd interest in puffing Julius Markham and his family in society. At last the duchess had resorted to tears, sniffing that he was the most wretchedly ungrateful of sons and didn't he *see* she was only being polite to the Markhams, only bringing them into the *ton* so that the alliance might be more bearable. Certainly, she sobbed, her delicate sensibilities had been rubbed raw at the thought of besmirching the family escutcheon with this marriage, but even *he* must see she was trying to make the best of it. At last Lord Charles had taken his leave, wondering why he still did not believe her.

He then made his way to the Burlingtons to find to his surprise that they had all gone to the Italian Opera. Mrs. Burlington had been sobbing only that morning over the disgrace Elizabeth had brought on the household, and he had comforted her by saying that she must not upset herself. No one would expect her to take Elizabeth into society now. Although he thanked a much mollified Mrs. Burlington for her loyalty to Elizabeth — although he did not think her very loyal — he had left wondering whether to remove Elizabeth to the country, where one of his amiable aunts might be prepared to take care of her.

But he had not thought Mrs. Burlington would show such courage as to appear at the Italian Opera — which was every bit as bad as Almack's, since it was ruled by the law of the exclusives — with Elizabeth Markham.

The Burlingtons' butler enlightened him to a certain extent. Mrs. Burlington and Miss Markham had received many callers after Miss Markham had returned from her outing, he said. So many people, very distinguished people, had come to pay their respects to Miss Markham and to wish her well.

Lord Charles decided to go to the opera himself. But first he would need to change.

Elizabeth was enjoying the evening, although her eyes kept wandering from the stage, searching the boxes for Lord Charles. What if he stayed away from her forever? What if he really believed her mad?

And then, without turning her head, she knew he had entered the box behind her. The air seemed to crackle with electricity — rather like getting a shock from one of those new machines people played with as part of a parlor game. You held a wire and got a brief tingling all over your body.

The theater was brightly lit, hundreds of candles blazing from the great chandeliers that hung down from the ceiling almost on a level with the boxes, as if the theater manager had come to the sad conclusion that society was more interested in looking at each other than at the stage and so would not mind the obstruction.

The Burlingtons shifted to make room for Lord Charles, who pulled up a chair and sat next to Elizabeth at the front of the box. Mr. and Mrs. Burlington preferred to sit in the back of the box. They heard the music that way without distractions they said, although it was really because they could fall asleep without anyone noticing.

Lord Charles covertly studied Elizabeth's face as she watched the stage. Her opera gown was a mixture of gold and silver with long tight sleeves and a deep neckline. Her hair was braided into a coronet, which gave her small head a regal air. He noticed that her eyelashes were very long and dark and tipped at the ends with gold. He felt he had been away from her for ages. He took her hand in his.

Afterward, Elizabeth could not even remember the name of the opera. She even managed to forget the horror of what happened shortly afterward. But in years to come, she was to remember that time he took her hand, how her whole body had throbbed, how the music had soared in a crescendo to match the quickening beats of her heart.

Could she even dare to hope that one day he might come to love her?

Lord Charles was experiencing slightly more

down-to-earth emotions. He wished the opera with all its silly caterwauling would finish so that he might find an opportunity to take her in his arms again. He did not want to analyze his emotions. He was sick to *death* of analyzing his emotions.

The wave of desire that engulfed him was nigh unbearable.

To stop himself from startling society by jerking her into his arms there and then, he glanced about the theater, looking for something to distract him from the intensity of his own emotions. Lord Charles did not love the opera greatly, and it proved as well for Elizabeth that he did not.

He found himself looking across at Lady Herne's box. She caught his eye and gave him a seductive smile. He blinked slightly, wondering how this raging passion he felt for Elizabeth should not manage somehow to convey itself across the theater to Lady Herne. Lady Herne was admittedly a splendid-looking creature. Old Lord Jamieson was escorting her. Then Lord Charles saw a shadowy masked figure standing at the back of Lady Herne's box and wondered whether a masked footman was Lady Herne's latest whim. Then the figure moved, and the light caught the dull steel of a gun barrel.

And the gun was pointed straight at the Burlingtons' box. Lord Charles threw his arms about Elizabeth and dragged her down to the floor of the box as a shot rang out. Mrs. and Mr. Burlington had leaned forward to see what on earth Lord Charles was doing, so that the bullet that had been meant for Elizabeth whizzed harmlessly over their heads.

The screams from the audience were drowning out the piercing voice of Catalani from the stage. Lord Charles scrambled to his feet and raced from the box. But it was impossible to find Elizabeth's would-be murderer. People were running hither and thither in a panic. He returned to the Burlingtons' box. Despite his fear for Elizabeth, he felt quite light-headed with relief. Someone was trying to ruin or kill Elizabeth. Ruin by possibly putting something in that lemonade and now kill by firing a bullet at her across the theater.

But one thing he was absolutely sure of was that Elizabeth Markham was definitely not mad.

When he returned to the Burlingtons at last, Lord Charles requested a word with Elizabeth in private and the Burlingtons tactfully retired but left the door punctiliously open.

"Now Elizabeth," said Lord Charles. "I think the time has come to tell me as much as you know about your uncle and about what went on in his house."

And so Elizabeth began to talk, her face turning slightly pale as she relived those two years in Julius Markham's home. Lord Charles listened carefully, and the more he listened, the more puzzled he grew.

Julius Markham's treatment of this poor relation was, sadly, not at all unusual. Lord Charles had heard many awful tales of family cruelty in the past. He supposed his own upbringing might be viewed by some as unkind. As a child he had hardly ever seen his parents and had been left in the care of tutors and servants. One tutor had locked him in a dark cupboard in the schoolroom for one whole day after a sound thrashing. The tutor was dismissed but not for cruelty to the young Lord Charles — for dallying with one of the housemaids. What Lord Charles *did* find odd was Mr. Markham's pursuit of his niece. He had struck Lord Charles as being a hard, avaricious man, and that impression was supported by many parts of Elizabeth's story. And yet, for all that, he did not appear a man capable of murder.

There was a long silence when Elizabeth had finished. "Pargeter," said Lord Charles at last. "What is his interest in you?"

"Oh, dear," said Elizabeth. "It is all very awkward. I should not have gone driving with him. You see, I thought you had rejected me, that you were ashamed of me. I see now that you had every right to be ashamed of me, considering my terrible behavior at the ball. In any case when Mr. Pargeter asked me to go driving with him, I accepted because I was angry and hurt. And Mr. Pargeter said the best way to allay scandal was to be seen in public as soon as possible. That *did* seem to make sense. But when we were in the park, he . . . he asked me to marry him."

"The deuce!"

"I pointed out I was engaged to you. He thought I was only marrying you because I had no alternative."

"To which you replied?"

Elizabeth hesitated. She did not want to tell Lord Charles of that sudden realization that she was in love with him. It might make him feel even more trapped. In a confused way, Elizabeth desperately wanted Lord Charles to fall in love with her and felt her own admission of love would somehow embarrass him and drive him away.

So she said, "I told him I was engaged to you and that we were to be married."

"Because you have no alternative?"

His voice was harsh. Elizabeth, overset with emotion and with the ordeal she had just gone through, began to cry.

"I am sorry," he said in a softer voice. "I will send for Mrs. Burlington. You have endured much. Leave things to me. I will get to the bottom of this somehow."

Elizabeth stretched out a hand and opened her mouth to call him back, to tell him that she loved him, but he had already rung the bell.

And so Lord Charles left the Burlingtons feeling low and dejected. He had not been in love before, certainly not this heady passion he felt for Elizabeth. He did not think he could now bear such a one-sided marriage as this was certainly going to be. After he had walked for a long time, he firmly put his emotional problems out of his mind and thought instead about the enigma that was Julius Markham.

If Julius Markham had somehow managed to drug Elizabeth's lemonade at the ball so as to make her behave in that frightening way, then it followed that Julius Markham wanted the marriage never to take place. That was the bond he had with the duchess. He had no doubt told Lord Charles's mother that he would do everything in his power to stop the marriage, and that was why the duchess was sponsoring the reverend and his family in society. Without the duchess's aid, Julius would not be invited anywhere. He was a dissenting minister with a vulgar wife and two vulgar daughters. Elizabeth's parents had been a different matter. They had been gay, witty, and spendthrift, and the ton had loved them.

Then there was the mystery of Pargeter, a young man who had never cared for female company. One way to find out what he was about, thought Lord Charles, was to track him down and ask him. "And I have every right to do *that*," he thought. "That popinjay can consider himself very fortunate if I do not call him out!"

The hour was midnight. Pargeter was bound to be gambling in one of the clubs. After running them all through in his mind, Lord Charles made his way to Watier's at the corner of Bolton Street and Piccadilly, that club famous for gambling, good cuisine, and suicides. He was in luck. Pargeter was already there, playing hazard dice, his face flushed and his eyes glittering.

Lord Charles stood a little away from the table on the other side of the room and watched. He thought that he had never noticed before the intensity of Mr. Pargeter's gambling fever. He was distracted from his observation of the table by the arrival of Bertram Seymour.

Mr. Seymour asked after Elizabeth and was obviously delighted to hear she was well. The news of the attempted murder had spread throughout the West End. "Of course, it was that uncle of hers," said Bertram. "It has come out that he is a Nonconformist minister, and people are canceling their invitations to that family right and left. Not because of the shooting exactly but because everyone now knows how badly Markham treated Elizabeth."

"I thought it politic to put that bit of gossip about," said Lord Charles. "I said that Elizabeth had been suffering from a *crise de nerfs* on account of . . ."

"Oh, I did not think it was you who had spread that around," interrupted Mr. Seymour. "Pargeter's been talking about the iniquities of the wicked uncle ever since the shooting in the theater."

"Odso?" Lord Charles turned to watch Mr. Pargeter again. "Tell me, Bertram, why do people suddenly want their poor relation home again, want them so much that they set out to destroy a marriage?"

Mr. Seymour put a finger to his forehead rather in the manner of Shakespeare and thought hard. Then his face cleared. "I remember staying with the Chumleys down in Sussex during the last hunting season. Now, *their* poor relation was a Miss Baxter, a sad, gray sort of woman, always put upon and made to act as unpaid governess to the young Chumleys. But on my last visit she had suddenly become 'our dearest Maria,' and the family was waiting on her hand and foot. Turned out some relative had died and left all the moneybags to Miss Baxter, so naturally they were all very anxious that she continue to live with them."

"But if anyone had left Elizabeth money, then she would know about it," said Lord Charles.

"Doesn't look like it," said Mr. Seymour. "After all, she's going to marry you. Oh, I do apologize."

"You know," said Lord Charles, "I used to pride myself on my charm with the ladies. I thought I was very clever to avoid the marriage snares that were laid down for me by several enterprising mamas. Could it be, *dear* Bertram, that I did not really avoid them? Could it be the young misses did not want to marry me?"

"No, you know that's not true," said Bertram Seymour wretchedly. "It's just — dash it all — well, you must admit . . ."

"She had no alternative. So I have heard. Mr. Pargeter, for example, proposed marriage to her. He was convinced she had only accepted me as the only way of escape from Uncle Julius."

"If that were the case," said Mr. Seymour, "I would have proposed to her myself."

"Perhaps I should let you take her from me," said Lord Charles. "I do not want to be married to someone who looks on me as a charity."

"Fustian! Miss Markham probably considers herself the luckiest girl in the world."

"In any case," said Lord Charles, "*if* Elizabeth were due to inherit money, it might explain Mr. Pargeter's odd passion. Markham is certainly not going to tell me anything. Nor, I think, will Pargeter. But wait a bit, Bertram! If she is to come into money, then why would Julius want her dead?"

"Because if she dies, then he inherits."

"Perhaps. I wish Elizabeth knew more about her relatives."

"Pargeter's just finished — in every sense of the word," said Bertram. "Looks as if he's lost a lot."

Sullen and white-faced, Derry Pargeter was busily signing avowals.

Lord Charles said goodnight to Mr. Seymour

and followed Mr. Pargeter out of the gaming room.

"A word with you, Pargeter," he said.

Mr. Pargeter turned around and stared insolently at Lord Charles. "I am anxious to get to bed," he said, "and have no time for conversation."

"Listen to me, Pargeter, you had the effrontery to propose marriage to my fiancée. I have a good mind to call you out."

The insolent look fled Mr. Pargeter's face to be replaced by one of fear. Lord Charles was a famous shot. "Miss Markham was unhappy," he babbled. "I was there when you called her your fiancée, and everyone knew it was the first she had heard of it. She only accepted so as to escape her uncle. Why, she more or less told me so."

Lord Charles saw a red mist of rage before his eyes. He could never remember being so angry in his life. He forgot that he had meant to try to winkle information out of Pargeter about Elizabeth's other relatives. He seized him by the cravat and forced him up against the wall. He shook him till his teeth rattled. "Stay away from Elizabeth Markham," grated Lord Charles.

"Leave me alone. You are spoiling my cravat," said Mr. Pargeter, his eyes beginning to fill with tears.

Lord Charles released him, dusting his fingers on his cambric handkerchief as if he had just touched something unclean. He turned and strode from the club without a backward glance.

The words that his friend Bertram and that Derry Pargeter had said seeped like poison into his soul. Elizabeth did not love him. It was now too late to call on her. He could hardly await morning to arrive to show her how indifferent to her he had become.

Chapter Nine

Lord Charles fell into an uneasy sleep as dawn was beginning to streak the London sky. When he awoke, he found it was one o'clock in the afternoon. He dressed and, without waiting for breakfast, made his way to the Burlingtons.

His bad mood engendered by hunger and worry was made worse when he found it was going to be impossible to see Elizabeth alone. The house was full of callers. She had become a celebrity overnight. Among the well-wishers were some of London's most eligible bachelors. Miss Markham was probably already regretting accepting his offer of marriage, thought Lord Charles sourly.

He decided to call on Julius Markham. Julius had rented, courtesy of the duchess, an elegant house in Hill Street. Its white paint, however, had been marred by someone painting in red the word Murderer in large letters. Someone else had piled a mound of refuse on the steps that the harried servants were clearing away.

Lord Charles presented his card with the corner turned down to show that he was calling in person. The butler, who had been rented along with the house, returned after a few moments to say that Mr. Markham was "not at home." Lord Charles debated whether to force his way in but decided against it, deterred by the sounds of hysterical female weeping from the drawing room. The womenfolk of the family were obviously suffering from their new unpopularity.

He walked away and had just reached the corner of Berkeley Square when he heard a voice hailing him. "My lord!" He swung round and found himself looking down into the round red country features of a middle-aged woman.

She dropped him a curtsy and said nervously, glancing over her shoulder, "I must speak to you, my lord. It's about Miss Elizabeth. But not here. They might catch me."

"Follow me," he said curtly, and he led the way into the gardens in Berkeley Square. He stopped under a plane tree. "Now what is all this about?" he asked. "Come, do not look so frightened. I will see that nothing happens to you."

"I don't know," wailed the woman, twisting her apron in her red hands. "You may protect me in this world, but you can't do nothing about t'next."

Lord Charles sighed. "If the reverend has been threatening you with hellfire, my good woman, pay no heed. The only man I have met of late who is certainly destined to end there is Mr. Markham himself."

"How did you know I came from him?" asked the woman.

"A voice from God," said Lord Charles.

"Please hurry and state your business."

"Well, my lord, I be Mistress Battersby of the town of Bramley."

"Battersby! Where have I heard that name before? I have it! Miss Markham thought she saw you at the Maxwells' ball."

"It *was* me, my lord. I be part of the plot to prove Miss Elizabeth mad."

"Ah, I begin to see light. What I do not understand is why Julius Markham should wish the world to think his own niece mad."

"It was something I think to do with that there lawyer man who came a-calling the day Miss Elizabeth was found missing," said Mrs. Battersby. "What a rare taking the reverend was in, to be sure. 'Find her,' he says, 'and when you gets her, put bars on the window of her room.' "

"Do you know the name of this lawyer?"

"Perkins, she's the maid, she says to me that he was a Mr. Thomson and that he had come to see Miss Elizabeth and that Reverend said she was out about the town, not wanting to say she had run away. Perkins was listening at t'door as she often does when they was talking. She says it was something to do with a Mr. Endicotte, an old man who'd left money to Miss Elizabeth."

"And did this Perkins find out where Mr. Endicotte lived?"

"No, my lord."

"Let's return to yourself. Why was your appearance at a ball supposed to give Miss Markham, and everyone else, the impression that she was mad?"

"Mr. Markham thought that if he dressed me up fine and put me where she might see me, she would cry out that she had seen this woman from Bramley. 'Twas a little thing, but he said it was essential that Miss Elizabeth herself should begin to think she was losing her wits. Then I had to give a bottle of chloral to Miss Patience so she could try to dose Miss Markham's drink."

"And what other plans did Mr. Markham have for his niece?" demanded Lord Charles.

"I don't know, my lord, 'cept I doubt if he'll be trying anything now, what with him being so clutch-fisted and not liking to pay for things himself."

"I do not understand you," said Lord Charles, striving for patience. "What has the miserliness of Markham to do with him giving up his attack on his niece's sanity?"

"I thought you, my lord, would know that," said Mrs. Battersby, "since it is your lordship's respected mama who is funding Mr. Markham."

"What!"

"Perkins says as how Her Grace called on Mr. Markham and as how Mr. Markham told Her Grace that Miss Elizabeth had mad fits and only he knew how to . . . to . . . permote them . . . bring 'em up, I think he meant, for he says that, like, Miss Elizabeth is sane for quite a bitty time, so a body most wouldn't know. Her Grace just wanted the marriage stopped, saving your lordship's parding, and so she says as how she will fund Mr. Markham and his fambley and gets them to all the right houses where they can get close to Miss Elizabeth. But Her Grace says this morning she ain't going to pay no more."

"It is not Miss Markham's sanity that is in question," said Lord Charles, so savagely that Mrs. Battersby cowered back. He turned a frosty eye on her. "And may I ask, Mrs. Battersby, how *you* came to let yourself be used to further this despicable plot?"

"Oh, my lord, he said he would pay me the reward money he owed me if I'd do it."

"Reward money?"

"He promised a reward to anyone in Bramley who could give him information about Miss Elizabeth after she was found missing. I saw her at the fair. I thought at first I was mistaken, for she looked so grandly dressed and all, but I followed both of you when you took her to your carriage, and I heard you call her 'Miss Markham.' I told the reverend, and he tried to get out o' paying me, but then he says he would give me the money if I came to London and helped him."

"So you were prepared to drive a young girl insane for *money?*"

Mrs. Battersby passed a swollen hand wearily

over her face. "You don't know what it is to be hungry, my lord, and to just want money to feed the childer. You just don't know what it is to be hungry."

Lord Charles had a sudden memory of Elizabeth eating ravenously in the breakfast room of Hatton Court. His face softened.

"Why do you tell me these things, Mrs. Battersby? If Markham finds out, then there'll be no money for you."

"Something uncomfortable *here,* my lord," said Mrs. Battersby pointing to her heart.

"Do not go back," said Lord Charles. "I will pay you enough. Come with me now, and I will put you on a stage-coach north."

Mrs. Battersby began to cry with relief and gratitude. He waited with all the patience he could muster while she tried to compose herself, and then he hailed a hack and bore the still-weeping Mrs. Battersby off to the City to catch the coach to Yorkshire.

The subsequent scene he had with his family resounded around the quiet environs of Grosvenor Square. In vain did the duchess plead she had acted only for his own good. The duke, who did not know of the funding of the Markhams, was appalled at the behavior of his wife and said so in no uncertain terms. Lady Jane tried to defend her mother's actions and was relegated to the stature of a schoolroom miss by the wrath of her brother. Lord Charles raged that the Dunsters had never contributed anything to the world and there was not one thing in his ancestry of which he felt he could be proud. Lady Jane, he said, was hell-bent on being an ape leader, for no man with red blood in his veins would want to take a family tree to bed. He thanked God that his own estates were doing well so that he did not have to live on his parents' charity. He then told them all he would see them at the wedding and, apart from that, the biggest favor they could do him was to KEEP OUT OF HIS LIFE.

Then he hurled from the house leaving a weeping mother and sister behind — and a very proud father. The duke heartlessly said he had not been so entertained in years, told his wife he was stopping the Markhams' rent out of her allowance, and took himself off to his club.

Still unaware that he had not eaten anything, Lord Charles erupted into the Burlingtons' home and scattered the remaining callers by demanding icily if they had nothing better to do with their time.

At last he was alone with Elizabeth.

"Well, madam," he said, after telling her Mrs. Battersby's story, "it may be that you are an heiress, and therefore you can no longer feel *constrained* to marry me."

"Oh, Charles . . ." said Elizabeth, tears starting to her eyes.

" 'Oh, Charles,' " he mimicked savagely. She looked so very beautiful and so very desirable, and he was now so very sure that she did not want him that he could have struck her. "Do not look so pathetic," he said. "Where does this Mr. Endicotte live . . . or rather where did he live, since he is now as dead as mutton."

"A village called Kayesmore in Surrey."

"Then I bid you good day, ma'am. It may be that I can reach this village before dark and so find out the address of the lawyer who holds your inheritance."

"I am most grateful to you. But why do you keep telling me that I felt constrained to become engaged to you when that is not the truth."

"Then what *is* the truth, dammit!"

"Oh, Charles, if only I could find the words . . ."

"Then I'll find them for you! I, Elizabeth Markham, want you, Lord Charles Lufford, for your money and your title. As a person, however, you do not exist. Well, damn my money and damn my title, and damn *you!*"

Crash went the door. Elizabeth sat shaking and feeling sick. At last anger arrived to drive out her sorrow. How could he be such a pig? How could he be so insensitive? She had been half-poisoned and then shot at, and now he had just discovered she might have some money of her own, and all he could do was stamp and swear and shout at her.

Well, she did not want him. There were plenty of charming gentlemen about, and no lady in her right mind would want to be tied for life to such a ranting, raving monster — a monster with seductive green eyes and a harsh handsome face and a way of kissing that turned her bones to water.

Mrs. Burlington bustled into the room and promptly averted her eyes from Elizabeth's tearful, angry face. "If the engagement is off again," thought Mrs. Burlington, "then I really do not want to know. Why cannot things be *comfortable?*" Aloud, she said, "Mr. Pargeter has come to call."

"I cannot see him!"

"I did not say you were not at home," said Mrs. Burlington, "and he promised to stay only a moment. He says he has an apology to make you."

Elizabeth's pride had suffered a strong blow from Lord Charles's visit. And what better way to repair that pride than by entertaining a handsome young man who claimed to be in love with her?

"I will see him," said Elizabeth. She ran to the glass and dried the last traces of tears from her eyes.

"I cannot chaperone you," said Mrs. Burlington anxiously, "for I am so very tired, you know, what with all the entertaining."

"That is all right, Mrs. Burlington," said Elizabeth. "Leave the door ajar. The servants will be chaperone enough."

Outside in the hall, Mr. Pargeter waited impatiently. He had been watching the house and had seen Lord Charles leaving in a towering rage. That had given him the courage to try to put another plan into action. Although he had failed to kill Elizabeth at the opera, the fact that he had actually tried to kill someone had made the thought of murder seem quite a rational idea.

Then there was his humiliation at Lord Charles's hands at Watier's. The fire-eating Mr. Anstruther, well known for his fights and duels, had come forward after Lord Charles had left the club and offered to be Mr. Pargeter's second. When Mr. Pargeter had said that he had no intention of calling Lord Charles out and that it had been just a dispute between friends, Mr. Anstruther had said in a loud, sneering voice, "I should have known a worm like you would take all sorts of punishment without a murmur."

Mr. Pargeter was now looking forward to killing Elizabeth. Not only would he get his hands on the money, but perhaps he might be able to throw suspicion of the murder onto Lord Charles. It was rumored that Elizabeth's uncle and family were leaving town that very day, so it followed that he could not contrive to blame Julius for the murder. Furthermore, he had a grudge against Julius and was glad he had been instrumental through his gossip in driving the reverend from town. For Julius had promised him, Derry Pargeter, every help in courting Elizabeth and yet had done nothing about it. Still, it was a pity he was leaving. People would be more anxious to credit Julius with murder than they would be to believe it of Lord Charles.

Derry Pargeter sighed with relief when Mrs. Burlington told him to go into the saloon. Either Lord Charles had not told Elizabeth about the affair at Watier's, or if he had, she did not care.

He studied her face intently, noticing the redness of her eyelids.

"You have been crying, Miss Markham," he said gently. "The shock of last night's shooting at the opera must have overset your nerves. I only came to apologize for my cold behavior yesterday."

Elizabeth gave him a watery smile. "I think you had good reason, Mr. Pargeter," she said. "I must have given you, unwittingly, the mistaken idea that I was unhappy in my engagement."

"Which you are not?"

"Which I am not," said Elizabeth, fighting down the tears that threatened to well up again.

"Why I am come, Miss Markham, is to promise you that there will be no repetition of my . . . er . . . overwarm behavior of yesterday. I respect you."

"Thank you, Mr. Pargeter."

He turned a shy, boyish look on her. "Furthermore, Miss Markham, London can be a very lonely city. I . . . I sometimes feel very countrified. I do not feel at ease with the Corinthians who swear much and drink deep. Perhaps my sensibilities are considered too delicate for a man."

Elizabeth's maternal instincts were roused. He looked so like a lost little boy with his aureole of golden curls and his soft brown eyes.

"No, Mr. Pargeter," she said gently, "I do not consider you countrified, and yes, London can be a lonely place."

"You are so wise, so understanding," he said. "I trust we can be friends."

"Of course, Mr. Pargeter."

"I fear that Lord Charles may not allow the friendship."

A slightly mulish look hardened Elizabeth's pretty face. "Lord Charles does not order my friendships or have any say in them," she said.

That brought Mr. Pargeter's head up. Elizabeth sounded confident and uncaring of Lord Charles's opinion. Could it be she had found out about the will? He must move quickly . . . but not too quickly. There must be no clue to the murder that would lead to him.

"Miss Markham," he said, "I would very much like to take you to see my dear aunt tomorrow. She is by way of being related to yourself, and she asked me to bring you. She is very old and has not long to live. She remembers your dear mother very well and has a miniature of her she would like you to have."

"I should be delighted to visit her. What is her name?"

"Mrs. Thaxted."

Elizabeth's face cleared. "Oh, how wonderful. I *do* remember her. Mama took me to see her when I was very little. She lived very near to a Mr. . . . Mr. End . . . *Endicotte*. That's it. An elderly gentleman. I am afraid poor Mama and Papa loved London too much in subsequent years to ever leave it, and so they lost touch with almost all the friends and relatives they had in the country."

Mr. Pargeter kept his eyes down. Mrs. Thaxted had died some four years ago. He hoped fervently Elizabeth would not suddenly remember *that*.

"I am so glad you can come with me," he said. "The poor lady will be delighted. Also, it may be as well for you to leave town for a little."

"Why, pray?"

"Because unpopularity is driving Mr. Markham and his family from town. I fear he may make another attempt on your life before he leaves."

Elizabeth raised a shaking hand to her cheek. "But Charles does not think he was responsible. He said that Uncle Julius was trying to prove me mad. He said it was because I had inherited money from . . . Good Heavens! . . . from Mr. Endicotte. You know, the gentleman who lived near Mrs. Thaxted. How odd!"

"Life is full of coincidences," said Mr. Pargeter hurriedly. "I think perhaps you should not tell anyone you are coming with me to Surrey tomorrow, Miss Markham. I really do not think Lord Charles would approve." He gave a light laugh. "May I dare to say that Lord Charles is jealous of me? Furthermore, it would be better for your safety if no one knew of your whereabouts. Think of it, Miss Markham. Just to escape for a few hours into the country, free from worries about uncles or murder."

Elizabeth *did* want to escape. She wanted, above all, to think about Lord Charles calling and not finding her meekly waiting for him. The brute! He didn't care a fig for her anyway. At least Mr. Pargeter was kind and sensitive enough to realize the strain she was undergoing. Wonderful to escape for a little.

"Very well, Mr. Pargeter, I will tell Mrs. Burlington that I had received an invitation to spend the afternoon with Sally Harper. We will not be away very long, will we?"

"A few hours only, I promise."

"But it is not conventional for us to travel unchaperoned in a closed carriage," said Elizabeth.

"I had considered that," said Mr. Pargeter. "The weather is fine, so we will travel in my phaeton. If it rains, why, we will put the journey off until another day." And I will strangle you with my bare hands in the middle of Hyde Park instead, he thought.

"Thank you, Mr. Pargeter. At what time will you call?"

"At ten in the morning."

"So early? It has its advantages all the same, for Mrs. Burlington does not arise until noon at the earliest, and so I can simply leave her a note without going into a lengthy explanation. I bid you good evening, Mr. Pargeter, and look forward to seeing you on the morrow."

Lord Charles arrived in Kayesmore to find that the only person who might know the name of Mr. Endicotte's lawyer was the vicar who had gone out to visit his archdeacon and was not expected back until late. He decided to stay at the local inn for the night.

He was now regretting having stormed and raged at Elizabeth. Once more he began to wonder whether he was as bad as his mother. He had never really tried to court Elizabeth in any way. How could he blame her for having accepted his hand in marriage because of his wealth and title when that was all he had really offered her. He had not once said that he loved her. Then he realized he had not warned her against seeing any more of Pargeter because that young man just might be trying to murder her. Until he saw the lawyer, then anyone at all even remotely related to Elizabeth was suspect.

He ate a hearty meal, the first food he had had that day. With his hunger appeased came the thought that he had treated Elizabeth abominably. He rode out after supper to the vicarage, but the vicar had not yet returned home. There was nothing else he could do but return to the inn and wait — and think about Elizabeth. The gnawing hunger he began to feel was not for food. It seemed a long, long time until he could see her again, although he would surely be back in London about noon.

Elizabeth woke the next day to bright sunlight. She felt wretched. The attempt on her life now seemed more horrible than it had immediately afterward. For a while she sat and shook so much with nerves that she could barely begin to prepare herself for the outing with Mr. Pargeter. Elizabeth was now more than ever determined to go. She would receive a miniature of her beloved mother and be able to talk about her, she would be out of London and out of harm's way, and cruel, unfeeling Lord Charles would find her gone.

She scribbled a note for Lady Burlington saying that she had gone to spend some time with Sally Harper. The servants were belowstairs when she left, and so no one witnessed her climbing up into Mr. Pargeter's phaeton.

Mr. Pargeter did not seem to be in good spirits and concentrated his whole attention on his driving. They were soon over Westminster Bridge and driving through the depressing manufactories on the Surrey side of the river.

Elizabeth was glad when they reached the open country. The air was warm, and a mellow sun shone down on the thick green hedges and arching trees. She tried to talk to Mr. Pargeter, but he shouted over the noise of the horses' hooves that he was anxious to reach Mrs. Thaxted as soon as possible so that Elizabeth would not be away from London too long.

He raced along through a network of lanes, and Elizabeth was relieved to see at last a signpost to Kayesmore, for she had been beginning to fear that Mr. Pargeter had lost his way. They arrived at the outskirts of the village, and Mr. Pargeter slowed his team to a halt outside a trim, square house that was set back a little from the road. It had the blind look of a deserted house, and the garden showed signs of neglect.

"I fear we may be too late," said Elizabeth. "Mrs. Thaxted does not appear to live here anymore. In fact, no one appears to live here."

"She is expecting us," said Mr. Pargeter. "She is very old and has few servants. No wonder the place looks run-down."

Followed by Elizabeth, he made his way up the weedy path to the front door. He knocked loudly. There was no reply. The silence of the countryside closed about them. The scent of flowers was heavy in the air, and the garden seemed to bask drowsily in the golden sunlight.

"I think we should try the back of the house," said Mr. Pargeter. "I fear something may have happened to Mrs. Thaxted."

"If something had happened to her," said Elizabeth reasonably, "then the servants would know of it. There is no one at home. I think we should make enquiries in the village."

"No," said Mr. Pargeter sharply. "We must at least try the back of the house."

"Very well," said Elizabeth. "I will await you in the carriage."

"Bless my soul!" said Mr. Pargeter. "I hear someone calling. Do come along."

Elizabeth had not heard a sound, but Mr. Pargeter's worry and nervousness were infectious. He led the way around the side of the house, looking over his shoulder to make sure she was following.

"Down there," he said excitedly. "In that little summerhouse in the garden."

He hurried over the uncut grass. "She is here!" he called. "Oh, poor lady." He vanished into the summerhouse, and Elizabeth could see him bending over something through the latticing that covered the windows. She ran to join him.

When she entered the summerhouse, she stopped and stared. There was nobody except Mr. Pargeter there. Shafts of sunlight shining through breaks in the latticing lit up the dusty wooden floor.

"I thought I saw her," mumbled Mr. Pargeter. He had his back to Elizabeth and was rummaging among the dusty cushions on a cane chair.

Elizabeth felt uneasy. A shiver ran over her. She should never have come this far with this young man unescorted. She half turned to walk back out into the sunlight.

"Wait," said Mr. Pargeter.

Elizabeth stared at the long wicked-looking dueling pistol he held in his hand. She gave a little laugh. "Where on earth did you find that, Mr. Pargeter? Never tell me that Mrs. Thaxted is a secret duelist."

Mr. Pargeter raised the dueling pistol and aimed it straight at Elizabeth.

"Good-bye, Miss Markham," he said.

"So that is the tale of Old Mr. Endicotte's will," said the vicar Mr. Forrest. He and Lord Charles were sitting on a flat tombstone in the church graveyard. Mr. Forrest had stayed overnight with the archdeacon and had not arrived back until almost noon. Lord Charles had had to wait patiently while Mr. Forrest enthused over the generosity of Mr. Endicotte in leaving money to found an orphanage. Then he had gone on to explain that he knew all about the terms of the will because Mr. Endicotte had made him a witness to it. "Yes, yes," repeated the old vicar, "I remember it all quite well. Julius Markham holds the purse strings until Elizabeth Markham marries. Then, of course, the inheritance will become her husband's. Mr. Endicotte thought of his bequest in terms of a dowry, you see."

"The one thing you have not told me, Mr. Forrest," said Lord Charles, "is who would inherit should Miss Markham die."

"Now let me think," said the vicar. He stared up at the fleecy clouds sailing across the blue sky. "It was to go to some boy. Mr. Endicotte had not seen him either since he was a child. Dear me, what *was* the name. Strangely enough I can remember seeing the child. A pretty boy. I was visiting Mr. Endicotte at the time. Like an angel he was, and still in petticoats. Long golden curls and brown eyes, an odd combination."

Lord Charles stiffened. "His name was not *Pargeter* by any chance?"

"Bless my soul. That is it. Derwent Pargeter. Mr. Endicotte was in two minds about mentioning the lad in his will, because it had come to his ears that young Pargeter gambled to excess. But I said . . . Good Heavens!"

For the good vicar found he was talking to the empty air. Lord Charles was already sprinting toward his carriage.

Lord Charles was consumed with gnawing anxiety. Why on earth had he ever left Elizabeth unprotected in London? Now Pargeter would have two motives. Money on Elizabeth's death and revenge on himself, Charles Lufford, by that death.

Lord Charles's well-matched bays were fresh after their night's rest. They sped through the village and out the other side. Houses and hedges hurtled past. Just on the far side of the village, just before the open countryside, Lord Charles rounded a bend and saw another phaeton swung across the road. He swerved his team, and the wheels of his carriage just grazed the back of the other. Fear for Elizabeth's fate would, nonetheless, not stop him from leading the other horses and carriage safely to the side of the road. A less-experienced driver might have been killed.

He slowed his team to a halt, jumped down, led the other horses to the side of the road, and tied the reins to a tree. He was just about to mount his carriage again when a ghostly voice seemed to call, "Oh, Charles, I will never see you again."

"She is dead" was his first thought, "and her spirit is calling me."

But Lord Charles did not believe in ghosts, so he shook his head as though to clear it, tethered his own horses firmly, and marched toward the gate of the house in front of which the other carriage was standing.

"Why?" said Elizabeth. "You must tell me why before you kill me. Was it because I would not marry you?"

Mr. Pargeter lowered the gun slightly. He felt excited and elated. The fear in Elizabeth's eyes was like a tonic. No one had ever looked at him with such fear in his or her eyes before. There was a lot to be said for this killing business.

"You set your attractions too high, Miss Markham," he sneered. "I would have married you rather than killed you because whoever marries you will have the control of your money. But since you *pretended* to be in love with that bully Lufford, the next best thing was to kill you. Now I come to think of it, it's the better plan of the two. I get the money when you die and save myself the expense of a wife into the bargain."

"*You* inherit?" said Elizabeth.

"Yes, I, my dear."

"Let me live," said Elizabeth, "and I will give you the money."

"Oh yes, I can just see that brute Lufford standing by calmly while you do so. No, you are better off dead. Where is dear Lord Charles? 'Twould be a fitting jest were he charged with your murder."

He is probably quite near here, thought Elizabeth bleakly. He was going to find out about the will. "I do not know," she said. "What did you do with Mrs. Thaxted? Did you kill *her?*"

"No, she died peacefully of old age. It's a mercy your late parents never cared to find out about their relatives." He raised the gun again. "*Now*, Miss Markham."

"Oh, Charles," cried Elizabeth suddenly. "I will never see you again."

"So you do love him," laughed Mr. Pargeter. "I like to see the fear and despair in your beautiful eyes, Miss Markham."

He took careful aim.

Elizabeth closed her eyes. She was all at once sure there *was* a God — not the God of wrath and punishment that her uncle worshiped but a gentle, benign presence. A great peace came upon her. She opened her eyes and faced Mr. Pargeter, looking at him steadily.

"May God forgive you," she said.

The gun wavered and then steadied again.

Mr. Pargeter's finger tightened on the trigger. There was a deafening explosion. Elizabeth's hand flew to her breast. The shock had been so great she was sure she was shot. But why did Mr. Pargeter have that amazed look on his face? Then Elizabeth noticed the deep red stain spreading across his coat.

Two strong arms seized Elizabeth from behind. She was beginning to struggle wildly when a beloved voice said, "It is I, my darling, my sweet."

She turned round and buried her face in Lord Charles's waistcoat. He rocked her gently in his arms.

"It's over," he whispered. "Come away with me. It's all over."

Chapter Ten

A week had passed since the death of Derwent Pargeter. Lord Charles had arrived in the nick of time and had shot him through a break in the latticing before Pargeter had had time to shoot Elizabeth.

Elizabeth had been taken to a bedchamber at the inn, ill with shock. By the following morning Lord Charles called to tell her that he was traveling to London to settle matters there. He had dealt with the authorities in Kayesmore and had seen to the removal of Pargeter's body. He had told the vicar and his wife to take care of Elizabeth. The landlord and *his* wife had also promised to see to her every need. His manner was gentle but rather remote.

Now Elizabeth had only to get better and wait — and long — for his return. She found this small village very different from Bramley. The tenants were well housed and well fed. The sleepy countryside stretched for miles around, safe and secure. The vicar Mr. Forrest and his plump and cheerful wife called daily.

As Elizabeth grew stronger, so did her desire and longing to see Lord Charles. She tortured herself with visions of him in the arms of Lady Herne. Why was he staying away so long?

She was sitting in the garden of the inn

watching the sun go down and the first stars come out. She was wrapped in rugs and lying on a daybed that the landlord had carried out into the garden for her.

Elizabeth was still reluctant to spend too much time indoors. Mr. Pargeter still haunted her dreams, and his ghost lurked in the shadowy corners of her bedchamber. The rattle of wheels on the cobbled inn yard below her window sounded like the arrival of Julius Markham, come to drag her back to Bramley. A light evening breeze stirred the leaves and sighed among the flowers. Would he never come?

Lady Herne was so attractive and so mondaine and so determined in her pursuit. Distance made Lady Herne seem even more attractive. Would Mrs. Burlington still be angry over the lie that she, Elizabeth, had gone to spend time with Sally Harper? Would Lord Charles be angry when he heard of the lie? Both Lord Charles and Mrs. Burlington knew that Sally Harper had had very little time for Elizabeth when they were at Hatton Court, and perhaps the very weakness of the lie would annoy Lord Charles. Perhaps it might make him believe she had really been attracted to Mr. Pargeter.

Would he never come?

The waiting was dreadful.

Was Lord Charles remembering all her flirting? Elizabeth remembered her own behavior with a sort of shame. But she had been very young and carefree before her parents' death, and there was no doubt they were a spendthrift, heedless, affectionate couple who lived very much for the minute.

"But they loved each other and were faithful to each other," thought Elizabeth, "as I would be faithful to Charles if only given the chance."

There was a light step on the grass, and a blacker shadow loomed up through the shifting patterns of the leaves. Elizabeth started up with a small cry of alarm.

"It is I, Elizabeth," came Lord Charles's voice, and she sank back against the cushions, weak with relief.

He sat down on the edge of the daybed next to her. The new moon rode out from behind the clouds, silvering the garden.

"How are you?" he asked.

"Better," said Elizabeth. "I still have nightmares."

"I saw the lawyer," he said. "It's a damnable business because you do not get the money until you marry, but on the other hand, it gives you a handsome dowry. You can have your pick of husbands, Elizabeth."

"Why should I want my pick?" she asked, straining to see the expression in his eyes. "I have you."

"Oh, yes, Miss Markham," he said wearily. "You do indeed have me. But I have been thinking about us, and I would not have you marry me simply because you felt there was no other alternative. I am prepared to fund you during the Season until you find some man you feel you can love."

There was a long silence, until he added harshly, "If you can love anyone, that is. For all I know, you may be content to go on breaking hearts until the day you die."

"I do not want anyone else, Charles," said Elizabeth in a small voice. "I want you."

"Why?" he asked.

Elizabeth summoned up all her courage.

"Because I love you," she said.

He gave a long sigh and leaned forward and gathered her in his arms. His mouth missed hers and landed on her cheek. He kissed her cheek, then her nose, and then her eyelids, and then his mouth found hers.

There was no restraint between them as passion crashed over them in great waves, and they kissed with such a fury that they tumbled off the daybed onto the grass. He pinned her arms above her head and looked down at her.

"I have in my pocket a special license, Elizabeth," he said huskily. "We can be married here by the vicar. No mother, no uncle, no, God forgive me, sorrowing Bertram."

"Why would Bertram be sorrowful?"

"Because the wretch wants you for himself, and I am jealous of him."

"Charles, do you love me?"

He placed his lips against her throat and said

against her skin, "I love you to distraction, my adorable flirt. Marry me tomorrow. Promise, before I forget myself tonight."

"Yes, Charles."

"And you will not flirt again?"

"No, dear Charles."

"I am drunk with you," he said. "Kiss me again!"

"My lord?" came a voice from the other end of the garden. "Are you there, my lord?"

Lord Charles muttered something under his breath and got to his feet and then helped Elizabeth up.

The landlord lumbered out of the shadows. "It's the vicar, my lord, come for to ask you about some arrangements."

"Very timely," whispered Lord Charles to Elizabeth. "I was about to forget myself. Let us go and see him, my love. Tomorrow you will belong to me completely."

The village turned out to see Lord Charles Lufford wed Miss Elizabeth Markham on the following day. Elizabeth's maids of honor were six little girls from the new orphanage, and Lord Charles's bridesman was the local squire. The wedding breakfast was a modest affair held in a field next the inn. At last the festivities were over and Lord Charles carried Elizabeth into his arms up the old rickety inn stairs to a low-ceilinged bedroom on the first floor. The raucous voices of children singing sounded from the courtyard below as the members of the orphanage lined up to serenade them.

"A very simple wedding, my wife," said Lord Charles. "You make a beautiful bride."

Elizabeth had been married in a white ball gown that Lord Charles had brought from London.

"Would you like us to be married again in London?" he asked, as he deftly undid the tapes that held her gown. "It could be a grand affair with the whole of society present."

"No," shivered Elizabeth. "I do not need another wedding. Today was beautiful."

"And tonight will be better," he said, kissing the back of her neck as her gown fell to the floor.

He opened the casement and threw a pile of silver to the children singing below. The singing ended abruptly amid delighted squeals as the choir scrambled for the money.

"My lady wife," he said, turning to her.

"Oh, Charles." Elizabeth hung her head. "I confess I am a little afraid. I do not know what to do."

"Come to me," he said huskily, "and I will show you."

And he did!

The employees of Thorndike Press hope you have enjoyed this Large Print book. All our Large Print titles are designed for easy reading, and all our books are made to last. Other Thorndike Press Large Print books are available at your library, through selected bookstores, or directly from us.

For information about titles, please call:

(800) 223-1244
(800) 223-6121

To share your comments, please write:

Publisher
Thorndike Press
295 Kennedy Memorial Drive
Waterville, ME 04901